# CONQUERING INDIA

## *Texas Temptations 1*

## Melissa Schroeder

D1570338

**MENAGE AMOUR**

**Siren Publishing, Inc.**
**www.SirenPublishing.com**

A SIREN PUBLISHING BOOK
IMPRINT: Ménage Amour

CONQUERING INDIA
Copyright © 2010 by Melissa Schroeder

ISBN-10: 1-60601-873-6
ISBN-13: 978-1-60601-873-6

First Printing: June 2010

Cover design by Jinger Heaston
All cover art and logo copyright © 2010 by Siren Publishing, Inc.

Printed in the U.S.A.

**PUBLISHER**
Siren Publishing, Inc.
www.SirenPublishing.com

# DEDICATION

To Shayla Black and Kris Cook. I cannot even express how much both of you have helped me through the last couple of years. Your suggestions, guidance and understanding have truly been a blessing.


Thanks,
Mel

# CONQUERING INDIA

*Texas Temptations 1*

**MELISSA SCHROEDER**
Copyright © 2010

## Chapter One

Some days, life didn't suck. All the traffic lights were green and all the shoes on sale were available in her size.

India Singer pushed the button for the fifth floor and wished this was one of those non-suck days. She'd had pretty bad luck for the last eighteen months, and the car accident she'd had that morning was just the cherry on top of a very big crap sundae.

Of course, once her car had been towed away, it started raining, and without any transportation, she was forced to run five blocks in a downpour. The conservative dress she bought just for this meeting now stuck to her like second skin and highlighted every extra pound. Looking at her distorted reflection in the elevator's brass plate, she wiped away most of her mascara. The small smudges that remained gave her a delightful raccoon look.

Thankfully, she kept her hair short, so getting it a little wet didn't matter. It was plastered to her head but with a few finger fluffs, it was passable. Sort of.

When the elevator didn't move, she glanced at the panel and realized she must have hit "lobby." She released an aggravated sigh and stepped forward to push the number five button. As she pulled away, a well-built man stepped into the car, almost plowing into her. He drew up short with a laugh.

"Sorry about that." There was a hint of Southern gentleman in his voice. Not Texan, but the slow, easy accent of someone from Georgia or one of the Carolinas. "Running late as usual."

"No problem," she mumbled, trying her best to keep her mind focused on her upcoming pitch. She already sent in the proposal, however this was the final sell. She would kill her best friend Delilah for a chance to land the annual T and J party. Her catering company, India's Traveling Feast, was gaining more customers by the day, but this would be the olive in the giant martini.

Granted, it was the first "annual" anything by the newly established, rapidly growing security company. Still, she could scoop up more customers at an appreciation party held by a security firm for their clients. And just in time to start pushing fall and winter holiday events.

"Hell of a shower."

The amusement in his voice pulled her out of her thoughts. His wide smile held genuine humor. The warmth in his dark chocolate eyes slipped beneath her chilled skin, and she had to fight a shiver. Now that she really looked at him, the man was gorgeous. Not traditional movie star handsome. No, he was better than a Brad Pitt or Hugh Jackman. He was sexy in a downright dirty way. Like he played rough and loved rougher. A strong jaw, full lips, and a slightly crooked nose kept him from being defined as anything but dangerous to her state of mind. His dark locks were in need of a good trim and sported fresh drops of rain, telling her he'd been caught in the downpour, too.

The dark red dress shirt deepened his olive skin tone, bringing out flecks of gold in his eyes. Black jeans fit his lean hips snuggly.

When his smile widened, she realized she'd been staring at him like an idiot. She cleared her throat. "You could say that again."

"Hell of a shower."

The comment pulled a snort and chuckle from her. "I take it you get accused of being a smart-ass on a regular basis, right?"

He gave her a look of mock innocence. "Never."

His flirtatious manner normally would make her nervous. Instead, she returned his smile. He had to be ten years younger, so there was no way he was seriously flirting with her. It was probably just a way for him to pass the time.

"I find that hard to believe."

He dipped his chin, a naughty grin curving his lips. "I'm often unjustly accused."

For a moment, she said nothing. Probably because every thought dissolved at the look he sent her way. A wave of delightful heat sped through her veins, heating her chilled body. Yeah, this one had "dangerous to the female psyche" written all over him.

Before she could respond, the elevator door opened, breaking the warmth of the spell he'd created. Her task at hand came rushing back, and her pulse doubled.

With a nod in his direction, she stepped out of the car and into the hallway. She should have been spending time in the elevator preparing. Even though she'd been ready three days ago, mentally reviewing all the key points of her proposal would have been smart after her rattling afternoon.

She saw the number on an office door and realized she was going the wrong direction. With a huff, she turned on her heel and ran into a thick wall of muscle.

"Oof."

"Careful, now." The same humor laced his voice as he slid his hands to her arms to help steady her.

She looked up at him and repressed a shiver. Goose bumps covered her flesh as his fingers moved over her arm. India cleared her throat, but unfortunately, nothing cleared the image of what the man and his talented fingers could probably do.

"Are you following me?"

He shook his head. "Although, it *is* a beautiful view to follow."

Now he was laying it on thick. Still, heat crept up her neck and into her face. "I bet."

"Since you can't see it, you can't judge." She didn't miss the deepening of his voice or the way his gaze dipped down to her cleavage.

Tell that to the extra thirty pounds she carried around, largely on her ass.

"What are you doing, sugar?"

She wiggled out of his grasp. "Going the wrong way." *As usual.*

With a sigh, she stepped around him and hurried down the hall in the opposite direction.

As she neared the door to the outer office of T and J Security, she realized her friend followed her. She tossed a glance over her shoulder at him. "You know, stalking is a crime in Texas."

"So is ignoring a beautiful woman." His gaze swept down to her rear again and then back up to meet hers. "Or it should be."

Okay, he was definitely flirting with her. She smiled, hoping it looked maternal, knowing she felt anything but maternal toward the man. "That's very sweet, however I have a big meeting right now."

"Imagine that," he said wryly.

She nodded to him again, opened the door, and stepped over the threshold. An older woman with some of the biggest hair India had ever seen—which was saying something being that she had spent her entire life in Texas—sat behind a mahogany desk. The nameplate on the edge of her desk read Judy Reston. She concentrated on her computer, typing like a maniac.

"You're late."

Her no-nonsense voice held no hint of warmth. She didn't even look up from her work. India stood frozen, stunned by the woman's rudeness. Before she could say anything, a grunt sounded behind her.

"One of these days, you'll remember who signs your paychecks, Judy."

The affectionate aggravation in his voice sent India's head spinning. She glanced at the flirt and almost jumped out of her skin when she realized he was closer than she expected. Only a few inches separated the two of them.

"What are you doing here?" She whispered.

"He's being a pain in the ass." The hard, quick answer from the older woman had India whipping her head around to face her. She was now studying India with a jaundice eye. "Can I help you?"

It took a few seconds for her brain to start working, but the man answered for her, "I believe she's the four o'clock."

"Oh, yes, Ms. Singer, Mr. Jasper will be right with you. As you can see, Mr. Thompson has nothing to do. Mr. Jasper had a teleconference that ran over."

Then she went back to work, ignoring both of them. India slowly turned around and found Wade Thompson grinning at her. India wanted to stomp her foot, or at least curse, but she knew it would have been extremely unprofessional.

"You could have told me."

His eyes widened. "I didn't know you were our meeting."

She raised one eyebrow. "Really?"

"Okay, not in the elevator. It wasn't until you started down the hallway in this direction that I figured out who you were."

And still, he'd continued flirting.

Oh, she wanted to die. Right there on the spot. If she could figure out a way to disappear, she'd do it.

She called one of the owners of the company a smart ass. Closing her eyes, she tried to pretend that she wasn't there. Maybe it was all a dream. A big, bad nightmare of how her day could go.

She opened one eye. Mr. Thompson cocked his head and watched her with a curious stare. "Are you all right?"

She would put on her best professional face and find some patience today.

India closed one eye and said, "I can't believe I called you a smart ass."

"You wouldn't be the first," another male voice remarked from behind her.

India opened her eyes and turned toward the other voice. Standing in the doorway to one of the offices was a tall, lean, blond-headed man who just had to be the 'J' as in Mr. Jasper of T and J.

She couldn't speak, couldn't come up with anything to say as she watched his mouth curve.

"And I promise you, Ms. Singer, you won't be the last one to call him that."

* * * *

Wade watched the most delicious blush crawl up into India Singer's cheeks and wanted to sigh. The woman was a walking, talking wet dream. And she didn't know it. Her confused expression and her total lack of self awareness told him that she had no idea just how sexy she was. And that made her even more enticing.

"Ms. Singer, why don't we meet in my office," Marc said, giving Wade a knowing look, then turned his attention back to India. "Would you like something to drink?"

She shook herself, as if trying to wake up from a daydream, and smiled at Marc. *Ahh, that smile.* The woman had the warmest, sexiest one he'd seen in a good long while. No coy or practiced curving of the lips. Every time he saw it, most of his blood drained to his cock. Hell, since he bumped into her in the elevator, he had been hard as hell. He was just lucky she was so unaware or she might have been offended.

"I would appreciate some water if it isn't too much trouble."

Marc nodded. "Judy, could you get Ms. Singer some water and bring it in. My water cooler is only spouting out hot water for some reason."

As Judy trotted off to do Marc's bidding, he stepped back and allowed India to walk ahead of him. Wade watched Marc's frank appraisal when India wasn't paying attention. He knew his best friend and understood that Marc's tastes mirrored his own. Marc glanced over and smiled. He lifted a hand to his chest and patted it over his heart.

By the time both of them made it into the office behind the delectable India, Marc had transformed back into the stoic businessman. Judy slipped in behind them and gave India her water, then left them alone, shutting the door behind her.

Marc smiled at India as he walked around the desk and settled into his chair. "I looked at your proposal and everything seems reasonable. Nelson Delgado recommended you."

As Wade sat in the chair beside India's, he watched her pause before taking another drink. If he hadn't been watching her, he'd have missed it. He wondered just what was between her and Nelson Delgado. Couldn't be an ex-lover. Nelson was seriously happy in his marriage. Shaking his head mentally, he decided to ferret out the info later on. Right now, his attention was all for India.

As Marc and their new caterer talked over her proposal for their year-end party, Wade drifted into fantasies featuring India. She was a joy to watch in motion, but when she warmed up to her topic, she became even more animated. Her whole body vibrated with excitement.

Lord, the woman had to be amazing in bed. All that passion had to play out between the sheets. And that rounded ass of hers. Wade would bet a cool thousand bucks that it would look pretty all pink from a spanking. His hand tingled at the thought. God, bending her over and slipping into her tight, red ass would be a delight he couldn't resist. He could just imagine smoothing his hands over her flesh as he took her from behind.

"Wouldn't you agree, Wade?"

"Huh?" Wade looked at Marc to find his friend smirking at him.

"I told Ms. Singer that we liked her proposal for the party. You know the food, the drinks. Then, because I thought you might be paying attention, I asked you to agree."

India's Caribbean blue gaze swung his way. For the first time since his teens, his brain went blank. He'd seen all types of different shades of blue, but he had to admit he'd never seen this particular hue. Almond shaped, with flecks of topaz lightening them, they were further emphasized by thick, long, dark lashes. The mascara she'd been wearing now darkened the delicate skin around them, making the shade stand out even more. God, he couldn't wait to have her under him, moaning his name as he watched her, those gorgeous eyes cloud over with passion.

His cock twitched, and he shifted in his chair. "Uh...yeah. We both liked the ideas."

One eyebrow rose sardonically as she curved her lips. "Really?"

He nodded and resisted the urge to wipe his mouth. There was a damn good chance he was drooling.

She gave him a look that was equal parts pity and amusement and turned her attention back to Marc. "As you can see, I gave you the ten percent discount we talked about."

Marc glanced at Wade again, his eyes narrowing before he turned his attention back to Ms. Singer. "Everything looks fine, and as I said, Nelson recommended you."

Her smile turned professional, the warmth seeping out of it. There was something there, and Wade was intrigued enough to make a snap decision.

"I had a few questions."

Both Marc and their caterer looked at him. A frown puckered her brow. "Is there something I missed?"

"Ah, I thought maybe we could talk a bit about the set up."

"The set up?"

"Yeah, there are a few things I wanted to talk to you about. And we want our lawyers to look over the contract." Which was a lie because they already had Arnie look it over. Wade glanced at his watch. "It's getting late and Marc and I have new client coming in to talk over security for their new location."

He heard a muffled snort from Marc's direction, but he kept his concentration on India.

"Why don't we have dinner tonight?" Wade asked.

Her eyes widened slightly. "Tonight?" She threaded her plump lower lip between her teeth. Jesus, the woman was a delight. Wade preferred honest responses, and he definitely liked that India seemed completely unaware of her appeal. It made her that much more tempting.

"Yes. That way we can wrap this up quickly. Marc and I will both be there."

Confusion clouded her eyes, but she glanced at Marc and back at Wade. Understanding came next. "Okay. I have a few things to take care of, and I have to clean up." Her lips curved into a self-depreciating smile. "But I can meet you."

He smiled. "I'll write down the address."

"If you just tell me the name of the rest—"

"Oh, this is our apartment." He handed her the slip of paper. "Marc here is a gourmet chef. Say, six? Will that give you enough time? "

She hesitated for a moment. "Your apartment?"

Ah, cautious. Was she getting the vibe that he seriously wanted her?

"Strictly business," Marc assured. "It's quieter at our place. We know all business we discuss will be relaxed and completely confidential."

"We security people are a bit paranoid about that."

Her confusion cleared, then she nodded. "I'll have to contact my assistant, let her know where I'll be for the evening, but it won't be any trouble." Again, she looked at Marc and then back to Wade before rising from the chair. "I'd better get going."

He took her arm and walked her to the door. "Do you have any objections to salmon?"

"No." Then she seemed to gather her senses and stopped. Turning to face Marc, she said, "Thank you again for your consideration."

Marc stood, and from the look he shot Wade, he had a few choice words for him when they were alone. He was nothing but charming to Ms. Singer. "This is just a formality, Ms. Singer. Your reputation is fantastic. And we do boast one of the best views of the Riverwalk."

She smiled at both of them, the excitement back in her eyes. "Great! I'll see you both at six." She slipped out the door, closing it with a barely imperceptible click. It didn't take long for Marc to let Wade know exactly how he felt.

"That's the sorriest display I have seen in a good long while."

* * * *

Marc watched his best friend turn to face him and sighed inwardly. The smile Wade sported confirmed his suspicions about his plans for the evening.

"Don't even think it."

Wade laughed. "Too late. Besides, after I plowed into her in the elevator, there was no way I could resist her." He closed his eyes and sighed. "That woman is built."

"That doesn't change the fact that she's part of the business community, a conservative Texas business community, that would happily kick us out of the club if they found out what we do. Besides, you can't ask a woman we just met—one that we are about to hire— to have sex with both of us."

No matter how much he wanted to. Damn, it would have been better if Wade hadn't been at the meeting. If Marc had known what India Singer looked liked, he would have made sure Wade wasn't around for the meeting. Now Marc knew he'd be listening endlessly to Wade spouting just how badly he wanted to take her to bed. Not that Marc needed help from Wade in that corner. From the moment he saw her in their office, Marc had wanted to do nothing more than strip her down, bend her over, and fuck her until he couldn't see straight. He didn't usually react that quickly to a woman. It was unnerving.

Wade opened his eyes, his dark gaze narrowing. "Why not? We've done it other times."

"Not with women like her. A lady. She's not a groupie from a bar."

"Don't tell me you aren't interested."

Interested was too simple a word for what Marc felt. His body still hummed from the encounter. Even now he could smell the moist trace of rain mixed with vanilla that made him want to lick over her flesh and ferret out where the scent was hidden. It had taken most of his control not to lean over the desk and sniff at her.

Her makeup had been washed away, and her clothes had clung to all her wonderful curves. Real curves. Full hips and breasts, with a world class ass.

"That ass," Wade said as if reading his thoughts. Marc shot him a look, and Wade shrugged. "I know your tastes."

"No matter what they are, we can't start up with Ms. Singer. First of all, she's a long-standing member of the community. Her company may be new, but if she knows Nelson Delgado, she's got some clout."

Wade settled in the chair in front of Marc's desk. "Yeah, what is with that? She seemed uncomfortable when you mentioned his name."

Marc bit back the groan of irritation and reminded himself that the two years Wade had on him didn't amount to much in maturity. Not to mention the man had one of the worst cases of ADD Marc had ever seen. "Not sure. Although, I think he might be related to her."

Wade shook his head and then leaned forward. "Either way, I don't think staying away is an option."

He released a deep breath, trying to hold on to his temper. "Aren't you listening to me? Besides, Ms. Singer is just not the type of woman who would jump into bed with two men."

Stretching out his long legs, Wade settled back as if in no hurry. And why not? There was no four-thirty appointment.

"Don't know until we try."

His jovial manner grated on Marc's nerves. Best friends through boot camp, the hell of Afghanistan, and now their own security firm, there wasn't anything he wouldn't do for Wade. But at the moment, he wanted to kick the shit out of him. Marc didn't need Wade dangling the idea of bedding the very delicious India Singer in front of him. Not when Marc fantasized just how wonderful her nipples would taste, how tight her pussy might be, how pretty that lush little mouth would look wrapped around his cock.

He shook himself free of the idea and brought his mind back to the task at hand.

"I'm not arguing this with you. But I'm making a list for you. It's Friday, and I'm not fucking shopping. You are."

Wade said nothing as Marc made out the list and handed it to him. "Make sure the salmon is fresh."

"Yes, sir." Wade rose from the chair and walked to the door.

"You know, she probably thinks we're gay. Didn't you see the way she looked at us when you said it was our apartment?"

Glancing over his shoulder, Wade smiled. "Yeah. But then, I used that to our advantage. This way she's not on guard. She thinks she's having dinner with two life partners."

With a laugh and a salute, he left Marc alone with his thoughts. There wasn't anything they hadn't shared in the last seven years. Beer, fear and a whole lot of females.

They discovered their need to share women when they were still in boot together. Neither one of them suffered from a lack of companions, but one particular night, after many beers and shots, they'd gone home with a woman interested in bagging two Marines at once. Even though he'd been wasted, Marc had known the night had opened a whole new world to both of them.

There was an extreme pleasure sharing a woman with Wade. Nothing had felt as right in the bedroom. Bringing her to the brink, enjoying her pleasure…it was one of the biggest turn-ons. Their time in Afghanistan further solidified the bond. In an intense firefight in the mountains, Marc almost died and would have if it hadn't been for Wade.

He knew a lot of people would theorize they were gay or at least bi. Marc didn't really give a fuck what other people thought, except when it came to business. San Antonio was still Texas, and for two ex-Marines trying to build a reputation, they didn't need the shit that would come from everyone learning their proclivities.

It pretty much doomed them to live as bachelors for the rest of their lives. Unless one of them decided to break the connection. For Marc, that would never happen. He didn't need or want marriage. Their one try at a permanent relationship with a woman had turned into a disaster. Add in his parents' wreck of a marriage, he'd decided long ago to avoid that particular insanity.

He shook himself out of his morbid thoughts and decided to head home. They only had maid service on Mondays, so he wanted to make sure the place was neat enough for India.

His lips curved when the vision of her came surging back. All that luscious skin, the full, sensuous mouth. His cock hardened, his blood heated. From the moment they'd spoken, even before he'd seen her, he'd wanted her. She had a quality in her voice that was comforting but at the same time arousing. Warmth oozed from her every word, and he continually found himself wondering just how he would react when he saw her.

Now he knew. His body still hummed with need and she had been gone over fifteen minutes. When she showed up tonight, it would take all of his will to keep his hands off India until they knew if she would agree to their arrangement. He stopped in mid-step as the implications hit home.

Shit, he hated when Wade was right.

# Chapter Two

India tugged on the bottom of her blouse as she rode the elevator to Marc and Wade's apartment. Her nerves danced the two-step. She glanced down at her sheer red blouse, straight khaki skirt, and sandals. Had she dressed too casually? It was a business meeting, after all.

Or did it matter? The deal seemed more or less done by now. If that were the case, her attire shouldn't matter, professionally speaking.

With a snort, she wondered why she was so concerned. It wasn't as if either of them would be interested in a woman her size or age.

She closed her eyes again as she remembered Wade's flirtation. Now that she knew his orientation, his teasing manner must be part of his personality.

She'd called her best friend, Delilah, who found the incident uproariously funny. Delilah could laugh because she never found herself in those situations. From graduating at the top her culinary class to every venture she tried, Delilah always succeeded. In the same situation, Delilah would have never thought Wade was coming onto her. Instead, she would have enjoyed flirting with him and left it at that.

The elevator door dinged open. Drawing in a deep breath, India stepped into the hall. Ceramic tiled floors and elegant light fixtures gave the corridor a rich appearance. In the last few years, San Antonio had renovated several downtown areas, turning older buildings into upscale apartments. And this one was the choicest of the lot. Some of the apartments had more square footage than her entire rental house.

She located their door and rang the doorbell. Before it opened, she tugged at her blouse again. It didn't cover her hips as she hoped, and she only further exposed her breasts. Not that it mattered. Why she kept thinking their personal opinions about her mattered, she didn't know. They were gay, partners, but here she was wishing otherwise and slightly disappointed. And she'd been doing that all afternoon. There were moments where she thought of both of them, naked…she shivered.

*Stupid, India. When are you going to learn not to want things you can never have?*

Just then, Wade opened the door, a smile curving his lips. Thank God, he'd changed into more casual clothes. But just looking at him, heat shivered through her. Her nipples tightened.

"Right on time."

She couldn't help returning the smile. There was something so inviting, so warm about Wade. She wanted nothing more than to curl up in his arms, especially if he was naked.

Oh, good Lord. She needed to stop. She would drive herself insane if she kept thinking about him in that way. At her age, she should know better. He looked damn fine in a pair of light beige, loose-fitting pants and a white linen shirt. She blinked at the sight of his bare feet against the wooden floor. God, they were huge and strong. When she realized she'd been staring, she shook herself, then looked up at him.

He didn't say anything, but she knew he'd noticed her study. His gaze swept down, briefly pausing over her breasts, then continued down. Her whole body tingled, heat surging through her blood, as his eyes moved back up her body. Odd, he paid more attention to her than most heterosexual men did. Her heart galloped like a wild thing.

When he finally met her gaze again, a little smile bent the corner of his mouth. The fire she thought she had seen in his eyes was banked.

Lord, now she was imagining things, projecting her own interest onto the man. Wishful thinking, pure and simple. She liked dark looks, especially on a man built like Wade. With him, she would never feel too big or clumsy.

She shook herself out of her stupor and smiled at him. "When food is involved, I'm always on time."

He took her hand and led her through the door, closing it behind them. Instantly, the aroma of butter and garlic surrounded her.

She took an appreciative sniff.

"Something smells good."

Wade's smile widened. "Marc's ability in the kitchen is one of the reasons I keep him around."

She smiled up at him, and they exchanged glances once more. His stare heated her again, and she bit her lip.

Oh, God, she wanted someone like this. Warm, funny, built like a sex god. Was that asking too much? He slipped her arm through his, and she had to fight the urge to lean into him. They strolled down a hallway that opened into a living area. Browns and reds decorated the room, the bold colors adding to the architecture. Ceiling-to-floor windows allowed for much light and afforded a stunning view of the Riverwalk.

"Gorgeous, isn't it?" His accent deepened, his sensual tone skittering down her spine.

She glanced at him as he took in the same view. The late afternoon summer sun lit his features, adding shadows and bringing out the gold rim around his eyes. They should build statues of men like him. With his chiseled jaw and pronounced nose—her gaze slipped down his body—not to mention other mentionable, incredible attributes, he was a sculptor's dream come true.

He turned to her, sent her a long stare she couldn't decipher. Almost as if he tried to figure her out. Her thoughts scattered, any hope of conversation disappearing under his attention. The man had her head whirling and all he did was stare.

*Think, India.*

She broke her trance and shifted her attention back to the windows. "How long have you lived here?"

"Marc heard they were renovating this area and bent the ear of a contractor working for the owners. We were one of the first occupants. It's worth every penny just for this view."

"It figures you're standing around chatting while I'm hard at work."

India twisted to look back over her shoulder as Marc approached. And she gulped.

Lord Almighty, the man was gorgeous. His ruthlessly styled hair now looked mussed, as if he'd threaded his fingers through it. A warm, sensual smile—which included a dimple—sent a sizzle along her nerve endings.

"You have your areas of expertise, and I have mine."

At Wade's quip, Marc's smile deepened. Her heart tripped a couple of beats, then swung into a rhythm that would surely kill her. They were both so sexy. What she wouldn't give…

*No,* very *wishful thinking to want them both.*

Marc came closer. His clothing wasn't any less casual than Wade's. His blue, fitted polo shirt clung to his sculpted pecs and lightened his gray eyes. The khaki trousers showed off his trim waist and lean hips. Her gaze dipped lower.

Great guacamole! The bulge behind his zipper proved that he was well proportioned. Hoping he hadn't noted her hesitation, she continued her appraisal. His feet were bare, too.

Realizing they had probably lived in different parts of the world and had perhaps taken on different customs, she glanced at Wade and asked, "Do you want me to take off my shoes?"

"I want you to do whatever you want, India. We like to relax at home and we want you to do what feels good for you."

Again, his voice slipped an octave lower, raising goose bumps across her flesh. She would love to hear it in the dark as he whispered against her skin. Even as she reminded herself that he was gay, her body ignored the warning. Heat churned through her veins, her nipples tightened against her bra. Since before her divorce, she hadn't been interested in men. It was just her luck that her sex drive finally reared its naughty head about the time she meets two gorgeous and sexy *gay* men.

She smiled, though it was hard with her out-of-whack hormones throbbing. "Now how can a woman refuse an offer like that?"

\* \* \* \*

Wade took another sip of wine as he watched the interaction between India and Marc with an inward sigh of relief. He'd been sure they would hit it off, but there was always a chance Marc's damned worry about their lifestyle would insert itself into the evening. Wade knew it was a valid concern, one he didn't take lightly. His gut told him that even if India turned them down—which he hoped she wouldn't—that she wouldn't spread rumors.

India was the first woman they had up at their apartment since moving in, and he didn't think that insignificant. Granted, he hadn't given Marc much of a choice but his buddy also hadn't put up a fight. If Marc hadn't wanted her as badly as Wade did, he would have invented a way to miss the meal.

She laughed at something Marc said. Her throaty voice slipped under Wade's flesh. Everything about her intrigued him, called to him. Soft blue eyes, the cute little turned-up nose, those fantastic breasts. He could just imagine wrapping his lips around one of her nipples, sucking it into his mouth—

"Wade?"

Marc's voice cut into his fantasy. He blinked and looked at his companions.

"What?"

"I asked if you wanted coffee."

"Sounds good."

"Thanks, both India and I would like a cup." Marc offered him a nasty smirk, but Wade didn't complain. If Marc wanted to be alone with India, he saw that as a good sign.

As Wade exited the room, he hoped spending time with India convinced Marc the three of them together would be amazing. Without a doubt, both of them would enjoy India.

From the next room, he heard her laugh again and smiled. Marc could protest all he wanted, but he never bothered charming a woman unless he was sexually interested. In business, they had their roles. Wade lured them in. Marc sealed the deal. Hopefully, it would be the same with India.

As he filled the coffee mugs Marc had set out, Wade thought about his next move. Marc had accused him of jumping too fast with India. While he wasn't about to propose they have a wild night of sex tonight—though he wanted to—he *would* pursue her, continue luring her. She was just the kind of woman they liked. Great sense of humor, smart, with a lush body clearly capable of pleasing them both at once. And maybe it would even mean more than sex. Given a bit of time in her company, Marc would see it.

He closed his eyes and drew in a deep breath. Waiting would be difficult, but he could—for a while. A short while. His refusal to give up India would piss Marc off, but Wade didn't see any way around it. He wanted India. And he'd have her, with or without Marc's approval. Once he had…well, Marc wouldn't be far behind.

* * * *

After dinner, India studied Marc and tried her best not to be attracted. It was difficult, especially now that he was more relaxed. In the office, he seemed…professional, distant, but at home, he was approachable…not to mention fuckable.

Holy Mother of God! She took a sip of her wine and tried to fight the blush rising in her cheeks. Just when did India Singer start thinking of men as fuckable? Granted, he was. So was Wade for that matter—big time. It figured she'd have thoroughly inappropriate thoughts about men who were gay. Especially both of them together. She had really bad timing. Or subconsciously, she'd declared them "safe," which allowed her to feel that attraction and fantasize.

"India?"

She blinked and focused on her host again. That intent stare of his silently demanded to know what was on her mind.

Smiling, she said, "Sorry. I'll warn you that while I'm a first rate caterer, I tend to lose my concentration in conversations."

He chuckled. "That's okay. I'm used to it with Wade. He knows the security business better than I do, but if you ask him to sit in a serious contract meeting, he can't stay focused."

"I feel my ears burning." Wade called out from the kitchen.

Marc rolled his eyes. "And he tends to hear me say things like that and miss important stuff."

India found their byplay fascinating. "How long have you been friends?"

"Since boot camp. Wade kept getting his ass kicked for that mouth of his, and I kept him from ending up in the hospital." He cocked his head to one side, studying her, as if trying to decide something. "How do you know Nelson Delgado?"

"He's family."

"Family? I've known Nelson for a year and I've met a large part of his family."

She almost snorted, but held back. Family? Yeah, like the Sopranos. Most people in the area knew of the bitter feelings between her father and his brother-in-law. They wouldn't be invited to any Delgado family gatherings. "He's actually my uncle, by marriage."

"Oh."

She sighed, hating to explain the issue. Her father despised Nelson for many reasons, but her marriage to his protégé had topped it off, not to mention their horrific divorce. She was just lucky her parents never held it against her and had been very supportive no matter what.

"My father has never gotten along with Nelson. They had a disagreement years ago, the family doesn't even remember about what, but my father has never gotten over it. My parents actually relocated to the Georgetown area a few years ago, so it isn't an issue anymore."

"I apologize if I made you uncomfortable."

She shook her head and smiled. "No. Most everyone in the area knows about it, so I'm rarely asked. You just surprised me."

"I don't know him well. I know *of* him and that he's looked up to in the community."

A point for Marc because Nelson was bad news all around.

He went on. "When he heard we were looking for a caterer, he suggested you. With his knowledge of the food industry in South Texas, we figured he knew what he was talking about."

His tone made it clear that Marc assumed she would be grateful, but she wasn't. She wanted nothing to do with Nelson and his motley group of hoodlums—especially Johnny. She forced herself to ignore her natural inclination to fill the awkward silence with something, even if she pretended she was happy for the recommendation. Her instincts in these types of situations were fucked up and had been for years. She'd listened to her instincts that told her to marry Johnny— and built his franchise of Tex-Mex restaurants. She knew better now.

India shifted in her chair and peeked through her lashes at her hosts. She wasn't entirely comfortable with the setting. Why had two gorgeous guys, albeit gay, invited her to dinner? Yes, they said it was to finalize the agreement, but that had clearly been done earlier in the day because the contract had been waiting for her when she returned to her office. And while she enjoyed the company, the food, and the atmosphere, she couldn't fight the feeling there was something else going on there. An undercurrent she couldn't put her finger on. She knew from experience that those things could drown a girl if she didn't learn how to dodge them.

"You want to ask something," Marc said. "I see it on your face. Why don't you?"

She couldn't tear her attention away from his eyes. Gray was too basic a word for them. A thin line of blue lightened the outside rim of the iris, and they were even more pronounced because he had eyelashes she would kill for. Light, thick and long, they framed his eyes in the most beautiful way.

"India?"

Oh, God, she'd been mooning again. "Sorry. You think I have a question?"

He nodded, one side of his mouth kicking up. "I know you do."

"Okay." She cleared her throat. "I'm a little confused about why you invited me to dinner."

Marc didn't speak right away. His gaze never wavered. "We wanted to get to know you better. We've been in business a year, but we're still building our name. One of the reasons for the party."

His answer explained the reason for the party, but not for her presence here, especially given Wade and Marc's relationship. Maybe that's why he'd intentionally dodged her question. Maybe he didn't want to admit his sexual orientation to her. It was possible, she supposed, they invited her here to give the appearance of one of them being in a heterosexual dating relationship. And really, was it that important?

"I see."

"No, you don't. Ask me what you really want to ask."

She frowned, confused. "Ask you? I just did."

He sighed, relaxing more into his chair. "You want details about my relationship with Wade."

"You're partners." In more ways than one, she suspected. No need to say more on that topic.

"Partners." He said the word slowly, as if savoring the syllables. "You think we're partners in more than the business sense."

Murky area. She knew the ins and outs of the San Antonio business community. While it was much more laid back than Houston or Dallas–Ft. Worth, it was still conservative. They would accept two gay men having an art gallery or a hair salon. However, folks wouldn't trust two gay men to handle their security. Stupid, but then, most of life was.

"You're friends."

There, that avoided the confrontation. India wasn't good at it, hated the sense of instability it gave her. She'd grown up in a family that constantly fought, and to this day she didn't like raised voices.

His smile deepened, but he said nothing, his attention drawn to something over her shoulder. She turned and watched Wade carry a tray filled with coffee cups and condiments.

He set it on the table in front of her. "You think we're gay."

Wade's bluntness kept her immobile for a second. She couldn't think of anything to say to that, but she heard Marc sigh. Again, she wondered why they thought it mattered to her. She wasn't a part of the rumor mill, and if they didn't want her spilling their secret, she could keep her mouth closed.

"I was leading up to that," Marc said. There was a hint of humor in his voice that had her turning to look at him.

"Really, it's your business, no one else's. If you're happy, I'm happy for you."

Wade laughed out loud. "Happy."

He slipped into the chair next to her and leaned forward, putting his hand over hers. Unlike other men she'd known, calluses roughened his hands, caressing her skin, sending a shaft of heat through her blood. Just as she did with Marc, she found herself mesmerized by his eyes. Where Marc's were hypnotic in their clear view, Wade's were dark and dangerous. When he laughed like now, the golden flakes were even more prominent.

"I'd be more than happy to show you where my interest lies."

His voice thickened as did her confusion. His interest. In her? Lord knew her body responded to the lust in his tone, and something was definitely up here. She glanced over at Marc. Her heartbeat sped up, her mind started to whirl. The intent look in his eyes had every bit of moisture in her mouth drying up. Those undercurrents ran stronger than ever, tugging at her mercilessly.

All of a sudden, her silly fantasies of having both men at once didn't seem so silly after all. Heat flashed through her, danced over her nerve endings, and knotted her stomach. She shifted in her seat, and her damp panties abraded against her clit. Pressing her thighs together, she tried to ease the erotic tension but only increased it.

*Gawd.*

Looking over at Marc, Wade asked, "Couldn't you just eat her up?"

Marc merely smiled. She couldn't decipher his mysterious expression.

She frowned at their byplay, looking from one to another. Very deliberately, she slid her hand from underneath Wade's. "I don't know what's going on here."

Wade opened his mouth, but Marc leaned forward, stopping him with a pointed look. Uncomfortable with the tension between the two men, India's stomach tightened further. Were they going to have an argument about her? Why? The perfectly wonderful dinner soured in her stomach.

After a moment, Wade's stiffness drained and he backed down. The undercurrent ebbed. The odd conversation left her at sea without a raft. What was going on between these men? From the heat in Wade's eyes and the way he kept studying her—which was driving her crazy—she wondered about his motives. Were these men gay or bi? Oh, Lord, were they the type who shared women, like in her favorite erotic books? Even as her mind tried to push the idea away, her body screamed for it to be true. She could just imagine what it would be like lying between these two powerful men, feeling their hands roam over her.

India looked from one man to the other. One was dark, sexy, with a mouth that promised nothing but pleasure. The other was a blond god, so serious that India wondered just what it would feel like to have all that concentration focused on her. She shivered as a double dose of desire speared through her body.

She was going to drive herself crazy if she did not stop these fantasies. Even if they were the type of men to do that, she wasn't truly the type of woman who could satisfy them. They might not realize it, but she did. Her marriage had proven that. She hadn't been able to keep a man her own age happy. She definitely wouldn't be able to keep two younger men happy.

"We just wanted to clear the air," Marc said easily, no anger in his voice.

Clear? She was more confused than ever, but India wasn't good with confrontation. "Ahh, okay, you can consider it cleared up."

She didn't know what else to say. While she understood they may not want people to think they were gay, especially in their business, she didn't know why they bothered denying it to her. Confusing. The whole evening was completely bewildering.

"How do you take it?" Wade asked, a naughty smile curving his lips. Her head spun with images of Wade leaning over her as he slid the full, hard length of his cock into her.

She cleared her throat, but nothing would dislodge that image— ever.

"Take it?"

"Your coffee."

"Oh." India ordered herself to calm down. At the age of thirty-five, she should be able to control her hormones. With determination, she offered Wade a wide grin. "Lots of cream and two sweeteners."

\* \* \* \*

"I know you want her."

Marc paused his typing on the computer when Wade spoke. "Of course I do."

He finished his task, then turned to face his best friend. Wade's mutinous expression told Marc all he needed to know. He wasn't going to let this go. Marc really couldn't handle this right now. Any talk of India Singer rubbed him like salt on an open wound. Every time she laughed this evening, his cock jumped. She was a bundle of luscious curves, all soft and warm, and he could tell she was attracted to both of them. But it wouldn't work. India was the type of woman who wanted forever—something Marc could not offer again. At her age, he was sure she was looking for more than a weekend with two younger men.

"Then why the hell are you being so stubborn?"

"Because one of us has to keep our business in mind."

"Jesus, Marc. When the hell did you become so damned uptight? You were the one who first suggested we share women. Why would it be wrong with India? She's incredible and—"

"Now part of our business life. It wouldn't be ethical while we're working with her. Or fair to her. She's trying to establish her business. *If* she agreed, imagine how it would affect her if rumors of our sexcapades got out. She'd feel the backlash, too. Maybe even more than we would."

The disgust in his best friend's voice did not deter him. "You act like we'll take an ad out in the *San Antonio Express.*"

"You know how perilous it is the first year. Hell, we almost didn't make it a couple of months. Do you think she needs us pressuring her? We are her first big event, one that could really have an impact. Think with your brain, not your dick."

"You want her as badly as I do."

Frustration crawled down Marc's spine. "I never denied it."

"Then what the hell is the problem?"

"I think that pressuring her right now is reckless and irresponsible. Jesus, Wade, we only have two weeks until the party. Keep your zipper up until then."

Wade studied him for a moment, relaxed his shoulders, though he still wore the same fierce expression. "I won't touch her for now, but I will pursue her once the party is over."

Marc hesitated, then nodded. There would be no reasoning with Wade. Once he was set on a course, changing his mind seemed impossible.

Wade speared him with another glare, then left Marc alone with his thoughts.

His buddy was right. Marc did want India, maybe a little more than was good for his peace of mind. She was a delight. Tonight, he'd wanted nothing more than to reach across the table, yank her out of that seat, and strip her naked. He could've had her moaning his name before the appetizers. He'd fantasized about sliding his hands over her flesh as he took her from behind. His cock hardened, lengthened. His blood drained from his head and traveled south.

Marc closed his eyes and tried to conjugate verbs in Spanish, but his brain quit functioning. And that was a problem. Being the voice of reason with Wade had been Marc's job since boot. It wasn't a role he relished, but one he did out of camaraderie, of love. There were times when all they had was each other in matters of life or death.

Now, though, he had to worry about Wade's behavior around India. Wade would never coerce her, but his recklessness could hurt their business and hers. And Marc wasn't sure he was strong enough to be anyone's conscience right now.

One thing he did not want to do was hurt India. Cherish her, love her body, take her up and over the peak again and again. That, along with fantasizing about sharing her with Wade, would cause him more than one sleepless night in the next few weeks. But he could not act on it. He just hoped that Wade didn't think that forever would last in a ménage. They had been down that road before, and it had left them both shattered.

It was not something he was ready to do. He didn't know if either of them could survive that pain again.

* * * *

India parked her rental car on the street in front of her house. Sadly, the compact was a step up from the late model car she normally drove. She just hoped that the damned thing worked when she got it back from the body shop. Her insurance was up to date, but the five hundred deductable she paid cleared out almost every last dollar she had in her savings. Even a used car was out of the question, at least for the next year or two while she built her business.

Getting in good with Marc and Wade would definitely help. Their client list had several huge companies in the area, and with a good party, she might be able to garner a few bigger gigs.

Unfortunately, she was interested in them beyond business. They were younger, yes, but both seemed to have their heads screwed on straight. A shame really that they were too young for her and, odd undercurrents aside, they couldn't be seriously interested. Hell, not that she'd know what to do with them, but it was a nice fantasy. Even a date with *one* of them would be more than she had since her marriage fell apart eighteen months ago.

Pushing away her disappointment, she stepped out of the car, locked it, and then started to rummage around for her house keys. She dropped her purse, spilling the contents out on the sidewalk. With a huff, she bent down to pick up the mess. A male hand slipped into view. Startled, she looked up and found her ex-husband Johnny smiling at her.

"Need some help?"

# Chapter Three

India fought the fear that tightened her stomach. Showing Johnny that she was afraid would give him a weapon. Her counselor's voice sounded in her head.

*Keep your responses unemotional.*

"You aren't allowed to be within one hundred yards of me." She stood slowly, trying her best to keep from touching him. When she gained her feet, she looked at him, looked past the tailored suit, expertly styled hair, bleached teeth, and remembered just how horrible of a bastard he was.

She knew she'd been an easy target for him. Working for her uncle as a restaurant manager, India had been overwhelmed by the attention Johnny had given her. She'd never had many dates in high school, even less as a working woman, but Johnny played the part of a besotted lover. She'd fallen for it, idiot that she was.

"I can have you arrested for trespassing."

She moved to walk by him, and he grabbed her arm. Her heart lurched. With more calmness than she felt, she looked down at his hand, then back up at his face. "I would advise you to take your hand the hell off of me."

The cold tone must have cracked through his confidence as he immediately released her.

"I just wanted to talk." His belligerent tone reminded her of the night she found him in bed with another woman.

She walked ahead, resolutely not looking back. "I don't. And the restraining order I have against you says I don't have to listen—not to mention the divorce decree."

The heartfelt sigh did nothing but aggravate her. At one time, she would have tried to placate him out of his pout. Not now.

"I had to close the San Marcos restaurant."

She paused then slipped the key into the lock. "I'm sorry to hear that." And sad, although she wouldn't let him know that. He'd use it against her, as he had in the past. She'd heard the franchise was in big trouble, but she couldn't let the fact that he ran their dream into the ground influence her.

"I was wondering if you could be convinced to come back."

His audacity didn't surprise her. When she found him in bed fucking her cousin Bunny, he seemed to think she should just forget about it, act like it never happened. Then he blamed it on India. It had been one of the lowest points in her life because she almost bought into it.

"I asked you to leave," she said without turning around.

"I know. I know." His conciliatory tone rubbed against her already irritated nerves.

She glanced back over her shoulder to see that he still stood at the base of the steps, a frown marring his perfect features.

"I can't help you. Leave."

Again, he ignored her. "I borrowed a lot of money."

"I don't care." She did, but not for the reasons he would think. That he ruined all of her hard work in less than two years' time made her ill. People she knew, many she hired, were now probably out of work. She cared about that, but she would never care about him again.

"I went to Victor."

Shock had her mouth dropping open. "Victor? What the hell were you thinking?"

He shrugged as if it were no big deal. "I needed cash fast, and Nelson wouldn't give me any more. Bunny left me."

She closed her eyes, fighting the urge to help, to fix whatever screw up he created. It was stupid to even have these feelings after everything, but they still lurked beneath the surface. Victor Martinez was Johnny's best friend from childhood and a leader in the notorious MS-13 gang. He'd kill Johnny if he didn't pay him back, and it wouldn't be a quick death. She opened her eyes.

"I'm sorry. If you don't leave, I'll call the police."

He stepped forward, but she shook her head.

"Don't mess with me. You already have financial problems, and I know the police can only do so much. But having your name in the *San Antonio Express* for harassing your ex-wife won't help."

Not waiting to see his response, she slipped into her house and shut the door. After sliding the deadbolt home, she leaned against the door holding her breath. A moment later, she heard a muffled curse and his retreating footsteps. It made her feel small, this fear of him, but she had to remember she no longer froze in terror. It was a step up.

It could never be the same, not after he had destroyed everything. Of course, when they first divorced, Johnny had left her alone. The problems cropped up about the same time as the business they built together, The Texicana Grill, started to fail. She knew Johnny had no head for business, and there was a tiny part of her who cheered when it started to fall apart. Still, another part of her died. It had taken them thirteen years to build that name, and within a year, the business was heading toward bankruptcy. The fact that Bunny left him was a bad sign. Her cousin expected to be kept in style, and Johnny was very accommodating to the younger woman.

She dropped her purse and her keys on the table next to the door, kicked off her sandals, and headed for the phone. Time to let her contact at the SAPD know of Johnny's violation, although it did little good. Once she got it out of the way, she'd sit down and get to work on the plans for Marc and Wade's party. She'd wasted fourteen years on Johnny, and she refused to let him ruin what had turned out to be a banner day.

* * * *

Marc shifted in his chair and watched the byplay between his best friend and India. He should have never let Wade talk him into lunch, but he caught him at a weak moment. Marc had just finished a phone call with India and had been wanting to see her, touch her. It seemed to be his primary emotion these days. Even talking to her on the phone left him hard. Warmth always filled her tone, comforting him. There was never a time he didn't hear a smile in her voice, a welcome that did more than turn him on. It made him want her for more than a night and that was dangerous to his peace of mind.

"So, how long before you get your car back?" Wade asked.

"It's working finally. Barely," she said as she rolled her eyes. "One of these days I'm going to have to buy a new car."

"Why don't you?" Marc asked.

"Everything I have goes back into the business. I needed a reliable van for events, so that is more important. If worse comes to worst, I'll start driving that."

Wade opened his mouth to say something, but his phone rang. He looked at the caller and grimaced. "Work. I need to take this. Excuse me."

The moment he left the table, an uncomfortable silence filled the air. Marc hadn't been alone with her since that first night. He didn't count phone calls. He had little to do with her. Wade, on the other hand, had been spending more time with her than Marc thought good.

"So, when did you and Wade decide to start your company?"

It was an easy question, one that many people asked him when making small talk. When India asked, it irritated him. While he wanted to avoid personal questions, he was perversely agitated when she didn't go in that direction. He pushed the feelings aside and offered her a smile.

"We talked about it when we were deployed. We liked to do recon, but really didn't think we were cut out to do life in the military."

She laughed, the sound of it turning the heads of a few men at nearby tables. Marc had to bite back a growl to warn the other men off. It wouldn't do any good, and he had no right but he wanted it. Which made it that much worse.

"I cannot see Wade lasting long in the military. He goes his own way too often. I'm amazed he made it out of boot camp."

"And me?" He knew he shouldn't have asked, but he couldn't help wanting her to have thought about him.

She tilted her head to one side and studied him for a second. "No. You aren't, either."

"I don't conform, either?"

She shook her head and took a sip of water. "No. Because you have to be the one in charge. I have a feeling you like being the one in command."

Her comments brought an image he had fought against for two weeks. India strapped to his bed, begging for relief. He could just imagine how her wrists would look wrapped in red leather as he mounted her. His dick went from semi hard-on to a full erection in a split second. He shifted in his chair again, trying to ease the pain. The fabric rubbed against his cock and exasperated his already out of control libido.

"When did you decide to start your business? Nelson said you had a chain of restaurants before this."

"Did he?"

Then he remembered their bad blood and regretted bringing it up. "Sorry, I forgot—"

"No, I shouldn't be so snippy, but seeing that it was Nelson's protégé who ruined my businesses, I get kind of sensitive on the issue."

"Protégé?"

She sighed. "My ex-husband. He fought me for the business in the divorce. I lost, of course. Partially because Johnny had my uncle's backing."

He barely followed the rest of the sentence. The term "ex-husband" was the only thing he heard.

"You were married?"

The words shot out like bullets, and her eyes widened at his harsh tone. He couldn't have been more surprised that India was married and divorced. Anger surged through him. Why? He tried to mask his feelings, but something he felt must have shown on his face because her smile dissolved as she studied him with a wary eye.

"Yes. Just over a year now. Well, it's been six months officially, but we've been separated for almost two years."

"I didn't know."

"Not something I want to advertise."

He nodded still not sure he knew why he was so pissed about it. He didn't know her then, and he knew tons of divorced women, slept with a few. Why it irritated him that India had been married, that she had let another man into her bed, made absolutely no sense. He just knew that he was possessive about her and everything dealing with her. It was an unfamiliar feeling for him.

"So, from what Wade told me, you have had a lot of responses?"

He nodded. "Yeah, but as I told Wade, you offer free food on a Friday night, there is a good chance most people will show up."

She laughed again, gaining the attention of several men. He ground his teeth together. When one particular cowboy gave her a little too much attention, Marc almost got up to teach that bastard how to treat a lady with respect. Wade strode back in, saving Marc from embarrassing himself. He looked at Marc and smiled.

As he sat down, Wade asked, "Did I miss anything."

India and Wade began to make small talk, and he couldn't help notice just how easy they were with each other. He knew Wade was over the moon for the woman. As always, seeing Wade charm a woman was a turn-on for Marc, as well. Nothing got him going like seeing his best friend talk a woman into bed. Knowing her the way they knew India made it that much sweeter.

Since Michelle, he had made it a point not to know anything about the women they took to bed. Now he wanted to know more. He wanted to ask her more about her ex, wanted to know just what the hell went on, but the look in her eye had told him she wasn't ready to talk about it. Was she still in love with him? Why the hell did he care?

*Because you want her.*

He pushed away those unsettling thoughts. Wishing for more than just a night of fun ended in disaster once. There was no way he would go through that again.

\* \* \* \*

"Yum," Wade said, leaning over India's shoulder as she arranged appetizers on a tray.

She turned to look at him. Too late, she realized their mouths were just inches apart. Her breathing hitched as she raised her gaze to meet his. Instead of the usual amusement, there was a hint of heated lust darkening his. His chest was against her back, and she could feel his heartbeat kick up a notch.

She wanted to lean back against him and purr like a cat in heat. Because the temptation almost overwhelmed her, she neatly stepped aside and turned to face him. In the last few weeks, she had seen or at least talked to Wade almost every day. He seemed to find time each day to check on her, take her to lunch, just something. And he was always touching her, which ensured that she would act like an idiot. India just couldn't seem to think when he was in the vicinity, let alone touching her.

*Because you want more than just touching,* her body whispered to her.

*Shut up.*

"Aren't you supposed to be mingling?" she asked as she crossed her arms over her breasts, trying to hide her hardened nipples. He was tempting her with that smile again, not to mention his clothes. She had seen him mostly in casual wear, but tonight he was dressed in a suit. The way it fit over his wide shoulders told her it was probably made for him. A man with his breadth of muscle probably would not be able to buy off the rack. And the color was perfect. Dark black, with a red shirt that highlighted the wonderful golden tone of his skin.

"I'm mingling." He stepped closer, his musky scent surrounding her. "I just choose to do it with you."

She rolled her eyes and stepped around him. This was not what she needed tonight. It was too important for Wade and Marc, and she wanted everything perfect. If Wade was wandering around causing her hormones to dance out of control, she would lose her mind and forget something.

"It won't help any of your business to be seen hanging out with the help."

He gave her an odd look and she knew why. Wade and Marc always treated her with the utmost respect. It would never occur to either man to see her as the help. She said nothing else as she turned away from the big hunk of temptation Wade represented. She flew into the kitchen happy to see everyone was working. She wasn't a pain in the ass boss, but she did like her people to at least put in a good day's work. She paid them top dollar.

India turned to head to the refrigerator to check on their champagne supply when she ran into Wade's chest.

"Omph." It took her a minute to untangle herself from him, his body heat warming her skin. She shivered as he slipped his hands down her arms and gently set her away from him. Her body reacted from the brief touch, her heart whacking up against her chest.

"What are you doing here?" India tried to inject enough school marm to her voice to put some distance between them. Unfortunately, Wade didn't seem to listen—or he had a thing for school marms. His eyes flared with heat and he seemed to move closer—if that were even possible. She could smell him. Sandalwood with a hint of Wade beneath the surface. The busy sounds of a working kitchen—the clanging of pots, the constant buzz of chatter—faded away as she stared up at him. Her lungs seized and her panties dampened. His sensuous lips curved. Images of having them glide over her skin, capture her nipple, drawing it into his wet, warm mouth flitting through her mind.

The shattering of a plate dropped by one of the wait staff broke the trance she'd fallen under, and she forced herself to take a step back. Drawing in a deep breath, she glanced at Wade and found him watching her, a flush darkening his cheeks.

Swallowing, she asked, "Was there something you wanted?"

He said nothing for a moment, a solemn look on his face. She had to resist the urge to fidget, to do something to break his intense study. A gush of wetness coated her slit. Gently, he took her hand in his and drew her fingers up to his mouth.

"There are a lot of things I want, but they'll have to wait until later." His warm breath feathered over her fingers, a rush of tingles spreading through her body at the slight caress. He kissed the tips. "Would you mind having a nightcap with me after the party?"

Everything in her stilled, her breath clogging in her throat. "Um."

He frowned. "Is there a problem?"

"Would Marc be mad?"

His expression cleared and he smiled. "I already told him I was going to ask. No worries."

She nodded. "Okay, but it'll be late."

With a knowing look, he kissed her hand again, then released it. She felt deflated at the loss of contact.

"I don't mind waiting on a woman."

With that, he turned and walked out, leaving her body humming and her mind filled with too many delicious fantasies to ponder.

\* \* \* \*

Wade smiled as he took another sip of his water. India stopped to talk to Farley Walker, a crotchety city councilman, and had the old guy smiling within minutes. Watching as she moved through the crowd, checking with their guests that they had everything they needed, he felt a strange twist in his chest. Damn, she was good, and while he hadn't made her his yet, he felt a jolt of pride at her competency. The woman was a natural at this. Wade was surprised she hadn't gone into the catering business before. He'd been to enough events to know this one was professionally run, the wait staff polite and efficient. She would gain some business here tonight, and he couldn't help being somewhat excited that he helped.

Wade tried to keep himself calm. His hormones weren't listening. Anticipation throbbed through his whole body. But it wasn't a new feeling. It had been a long couple of weeks with India, trying to keep his hands to himself. Since he had promised Marc not to take her to bed until after their party, he had to remain somewhat platonic. He used the time with her to make sure India was aware of him. His plan worked almost too well. His cock still twitched from their encounter in the kitchen. Jesus, the woman had him shaking, ready to come in his pants, and she barely touched him.

He couldn't wait to get her in bed and beneath him. Closing his eyes, he thought of what it would be like to sink into her soft, tight pussy, feel those muscles ripple over his cock.

"Where have you been?" Marc asked, breaking into Wade's pleasant fantasy.

Wade didn't even try and hide his smile. "Talkin' to India."

Marc rolled his eyes and grabbed a drink off a passing waiter. He said nothing for a few moments, and Wade looked over at him. He followed Marc's line of vision and knew he was watching India.

Marc looked at Wade. "I told you to leave her alone."

"I am, until the party is over."

"You're going to end up hurting her. She's a forever kind of woman."

He cocked his head to the side and studied his friend. "How do you know that? From what she's told me, she isn't interested in marriage."

"Maybe not, but she hasn't dated anyone since her divorce."

"How do you know that?"

"She mentioned it."

Wade frowned. "When did you talk to her about that?"

"Yesterday at lunch."

That surprised Wade, but he didn't let it show. Instead, he shrugged, trying to fight the gnawing in his stomach. Wade knew he was right about India. "Maybe I've decided to become a forever kind of guy."

Marc's eyebrows shot up to his hairline. "Really? When did this come about?"

Wade shrugged again, not entirely comfortable about his feelings for India. He just knew he wanted her and her only. It was a first for him.

"Not sure. Just know that I want her."

Marc sighed, the sound of it so weary, it worried Wade. His best friend had been worrying Wade for several months...really since that bitch Michelle had torn Marc's heart in two, leaving both Marc and Wade unsure of their relationship. It had only been weeks before they left that she offered up her ultimatum to Marc, leaving him without a whole heart and on edge. That wasn't the way to head out. After they returned from deployment, Marc threw himself into work, and they continued their usual hookups, but something had changed. And until India dropped into their world, he hadn't known what it was. Marc had been going through the motions, sating his lust with the women they shared, but he pulled himself back from both Wade and any woman they brought to bed.

Until India. She had gotten under his skin.

"Does she know about what we do?" Marc's voice changed, deepened, and Wade knew he had been right about Marc's feelings for India. His best friend not only wanted her, he needed her.

"Not sure. She knows something is up. I did find out she reads some very naughty stuff."

Marc whipped his head around, and Wade wanted to shout with happiness at the heat he saw in his best friend's eyes.

"What kind of naughty stuff?"

"Erotic romances...with two guys and a girl."

Marc shook his head and turned his attention back to the milling crowd. "I don't believe you."

"I'm serious. Remember the bag she had the other day at lunch? After you left, the bag toppled over on the table, and I noticed the title." He could still remember the way she stammered as she shoved the book back in the bag. Finding out the book had been a ménage left his dick hard and his knees weak. "I looked it up later and was amazed when I saw the subject matter."

Marc slanted him a look. "Doesn't mean she would be into it."

Wade didn't argue because he knew Marc said it more for himself than for Wade.

"I'm taking her home tonight, so don't look for me until morning."

The hardening of Marc's jaw was the only sign of his reaction. With a quick, sharp nod, Marc stalked off, but Wade hoped he planted enough images to keep his friend up for the night. Because, like it or not, tonight Wade planned on making Ms. India Singer his. Marc would have to decide if he planned on joining them.

# Chapter Four

Marc watched India as she moved through the milling crowd and tried to ignore the warmth growing in his chest. It was hard to overlook her even in a crowded room. There was something about her, a light from within that drew him whenever she was near. From the moment he met her, he had been drawn to her. Wade had that much right. But he knew there were lines he couldn't cross, and bedding someone he saw as an employee was one of those lines.

She noticed him watching her, smiled, and started in his direction. He should be used to the way his heart sped up and the way his palms started to sweat…but he wasn't. Every time he talked to her over the last few weeks, he had the same reaction. And it was getting worse.

"Marc." Even over the din of partygoers he could hear the warmth in her voice. It slid under his flesh, curled around his heart. "I hope you're pleased with everything."

He smiled. "Of course. How could I not be?"

A cute blush worked its way up into her cheeks. Over the last few weeks, he realized that India wasn't used to compliments. It was so odd because he had never seen a more competent businesswoman. She had been thorough and confident in her bid. But she seemed completely befuddled when she was complimented.

"That's good." He could barely hear her.

"Making a lot of good contacts?"

She nodded, but her gaze moved over the crowd.

"If you need to get back…"

She shook her head. "No. It's just that...I feel as if someone is watching me." She shrugged. "I think I am just a little crazy because of today. So many details I wanted to get perfect for you and Wade."

"It is perfect."

She smiled, and opened her mouth to respond, but snapped it shut. Any color she had drained from her face.

"India?"

"India. It's a pleasure to see you here."

Marc turned at the sound of Nelson Delgado behind him. It showed just how distracted he was that he hadn't noticed Nelson had been approaching them.

"Nelson." India didn't look that happy to see her uncle by marriage. In fact there was a mixture of disgust and fear that passed over her expression before she schooled her features. She was afraid of her uncle?

"Nelson, I'm happy to see that you could make it tonight."

Nelson moved his attention away from India to look at Marc. "I would never miss an invitation from T and J, especially when catered by India. Top class."

Marc waited for India to thank him, but she said nothing. He glanced over to find her gaze moving back to the crowd as if looking for someone. Wade? Did she feel that if Nelson were to try something that he couldn't protect her?

"I agree. India does have a special gift."

"I was wondering if you would be interested in catering an event for me."

Slowly, she turned her attention back to Nelson, her eyes so cold that Marc was amazed the temperature in the room hadn't dropped twenty degrees.

"I don't think so."

Nelson gave her a smile that sent ice sliding down Marc's back. Before Marc knew what he was doing, he stepped closer to her.

"Come now, you don't know what day it is, or for what."

"Nelson, when I said no, I meant it. I appreciate any recommendations you might have given me, but I am doing this on my own. And I'm not going to handle Bunny's birthday."

A flash of anger lit Nelson's eyes before it dissolved into a patronizing look. "You know where to reach me if you change your mind. Thank you again, Marc. My wife and I are having a wonderful time."

He turned and walked away, people moving out of his way without him saying a word. Marc glanced at India, and he could tell nothing from her expression. It was so unlike India, so frozen. He always thought of her as a colorful person, but it seemed that Nelson zapped every bit of that out of her.

"India?"

She shook herself as if she had forgotten where she was. When she finally met his gaze, she had hidden whatever emotion she'd been feeling. The smile she offered had no warmth.

"I'm sorry about that. Nelson, if you know how he handles business, you know he is a bit of a control freak. I just want to make it on my own."

He hated the professional smile she offered him. It was as if she were a different woman than the one he had been talking to the last few weeks.

"You don't have to explain it to me. I'll let you in on a little secret."

He waited for her to look over at him, her eyes lighting with interest, some of the coldness already dissolving from her expression. "What?"

Marc leaned closer, which was a mistake because he could smell her vanilla scent. His mouth watered, his blood went hot. He pushed away the urge to grab her and drag her off to the nearest flat surface.

"Marc?" Her voice was a little breathless as if she felt it, too. Just knowing she might be aroused sent a shot of heat straight to his dick.

"What?"

"The secret?"

For a second, he said nothing, couldn't. His brain seemed to shut down but for one thought…kiss her.

Then, a loud jolt of laughter had him jerking away. He closed his eyes and counted backwards. Then he opened his eyes to find India staring at him as if he'd grown another head.

"Sorry. The secret is my folks come from a lot of money. They wanted to front us the capital we needed to start the business."

"And you said no."

He nodded. "It would come with strings attached and neither Wade nor I wanted that."

A look of understanding passed over her expression. "The price is too high."

He knew from her tone that she spoke of her own experience.

He nodded, then looked away. He couldn't deal with the intimacy of the situation, the way she looked up at him. It made him want things that were never going to happen. And he did want them, more than he ever did. Not even with Michelle had he wanted it this much. Marc knew that with India it would be hot. He hadn't even kissed her and he knew she would be delicious. Taking her with Wade, watching her give over to pleasure…that would be the ultimate thrill. But there was something else there, something that was a little too close to an emotion he didn't want to deal with.

"Well, I need to get back to work."

"Yes."

When he said nothing more, she turned away, but he couldn't let her go with a curt comment. "India." She looked over her shoulder at him. "The party is amazing. Thank you."

She gave him a brilliant smile, her eyes lighting up. "Thank you. I aim to please."

Marc watched her walk away and tried not to think of just how he wanted to take her to bed and put that claim to the test.

* * * *

India parked her clunker on the curb in front of her rental house and watched Wade pull his truck in behind her. A delicious little tremor curled in her stomach even as she reminded herself this was just a drink between friends. By the time she slid out of the car, Wade was there to hold her hand and shut her door. They walked around her car, then side by side to her porch.

"You live here alone?" he asked as he took the keys from her and unlocked her door. It was a gesture that should irritate her, as if she couldn't unlock her own door, but his mannerisms told her that he had been raised in the South. And there was a little part of her heart that did somersaults each time he held the chair for her.

"I don't think I could handle a roommate. I do a lot of work from home and at odd hours. I think anyone living with me would be ready to kill me after a few weeks in the same house."

He waited for her to step over the threshold then followed her in. "I doubt anyone would want to kill you."

Before she could answer that, he shut the door, the definite click sounded so loud in her quiet house. As they made their way to her kitchen, she thanked God she actually cleaned her house a few days ago. After her weeks of contact with Wade, she had to find some way to work her frustrations out. Her house hadn't been this clean since she moved in.

"I don't have much to drink," she said with an apologetic smile. "But I do have some beer and a nice Riesling."

When he said nothing, she looked over her shoulder. The gentle, sexy smile curving his lips had her breath clogging her throat.

"I didn't come here for a drink."

She frowned at him, or tried, but wasn't quite able to achieve it. Her body shimmered little sparks of heat, her nipples so hard, she was amazed they didn't poke holes in her cotton bra. She didn't even want to think about the condition of her panties.

"W-why did you come?"

Lust swirled in his gaze, his smile widened. With measured steps, he approached her and backed her up against her table. Everything in her stilled, except for her heart. It beat out of control. He rested his hands on her hips.

"I came here to be with you."

Images of having him in her bed, naked, his cock thrusting into her sent her head spinning. She shook it, trying to bring some sanity back.

"Be with me?"

He stepped closer, pulling her up against him. There was no doubting his arousal. She could feel his long, hard shaft against her sex. Wetness seeped from her slit, her clit throbbed.

"I want you." He dipped his head and stole a kiss, sliding the tip of his tongue over her lips. "If I don't have you, I'm pretty sure I could go out of my ever-loving mind."

India shivered as Wade continued to press soft, wet kisses on her mouth. After a few moments, he pulled back and looked at her, a frown marring his gorgeous features. Of course, it just made him even more attractive to her.

"Is there something wrong?"

She shook her head, still trying to separate her fantasy life and her real life. They seemed to have bled into each other, and she didn't know what to think.

"N-no, I'm just..."

How did she explain that she couldn't imagine that a man like him would want to have a woman like her without sounding pathetic?

"I didn't read you wrong, did I? I was sure you wanted this as much as I did."

She suppressed a snort. There was no way on earth he wanted her more than she wanted him. Life just didn't work that way for India Rae Singer.

"No. You read me right, and I do want you...but I thought you were with Marc."

"I thought I could get away without talking about this, but I guess not."

"Are you and Marc lovers?"

He shook his head. "I'll not tell you that something doesn't pass between us at times, but it is always while we're sharing a woman."

"Sharing?" She gulped and looked up into his eyes. He hadn't moved away, still held her hips. The sincerity in his gaze told her he wasn't kidding. Good Lord, it *was* just like one of her fantasy books.

"We share women."

He said it as if she didn't understand. Just the thought of being taken by both men, being at their mercy as they pleasured her again and again sent a bolt of heat blazing through her blood.

"But...you're here by yourself."

He grimaced. "Marc is dealing with some issues. I couldn't wait."

What did that mean? That Marc didn't want her, but Wade did?

She didn't have time to contemplate the answers to those questions. Wade pulled her more tightly against him. "Enough about my partner. What I want to talk about is getting you naked."

Need crawled through her, causing a flash wave of heated pleasure to dance over her flesh. She wanted this, needed it. The craving for him grew each time she saw him. Never in her life had she needed a man like this. Her whole body throbbed, yearned. The tension grew thicker, her breathing shuddered. As she looked up at him, she found him watching her, his intent gaze waiting, full of hope.

He was younger, way out of her league, and normally she wouldn't do this. But right now, she didn't give a damn. She didn't want to be the good girl tonight. Tonight, India Singer wanted to be the bad girl, the one who always did the things she wanted.

India offered him what she hoped was a sultry smile, and her heart jumped when his own widened.

"As long as you're naked, too."

* * * *

Wade's head spun as most of the blood drained from it and shot straight to his cock. When she hesitated, his heart stopped. He worried that she didn't want him, but only he and Marc together. If that was her thinking, that she only wanted a thrill for the night, Wade would have forced himself to offer it and walk away after. But, thankfully, that hadn't happened.

With a whoop, he leaned down and picked her up. Her surprised gasp was so erotic, his knees almost buckled. She wasn't a virgin, but she seemed so unaware of her sexuality, as if she had no idea just what she did to him.

"Wade, put me down."

He could hear the embarrassment in her voice and he smiled at her blush. "No, way. I've been wanting to get my hands on you since I ran into you in the elevator."

Her brows rose. "You have not."

He made his way into her bedroom and smiled when he saw her bed. Lordy, she was a bundle of surprises. The room was relaxing, draped in cool, soothing colors, but the massive king-sized bed was what caught his attention. He could barely make it around it since it took up most of the room. With a laugh, he dropped her on the mattress and then followed her down on it. She squeaked then moaned when he pressed his mouth to hers, sliding his tongue in for a taste.

Damn, but the woman was a morsel. Sweet, tangy, filled with so much passion, it took his breath away.

She shivered against him, her nipples biting through the fabric and into his chest. When he pulled away, resting his weight on his hands, he looked down at her. She was in pleasant disarray, her curls a mess, her lips swollen from his kiss, and the most adorable blush still burning her face.

Jesus, once he buried his cock deep inside of her, he didn't know if he would last more than a few strokes.

"God, woman, you drive me crazy." He meant to keep the tone light, but he failed. His voice had deepened, speaking his need for her even if he didn't say the words. He couldn't help it. He'd been truthful with her. He had wanted her the first time they met, and it had been a test of his control not to take her before the party. But he had kept his promise, and now he planned on getting his just rewards.

He rested his body alongside hers, undoing first her vest then her blouse. The skin beneath it was soft as a feather, golden as the sun.

He slipped his fingers beneath the bra, and she shuddered. She had a front enclosure on her sensible cotton bra. With ease, he undid the snap, and her breasts poured out.

"Holy Mother of God." He had known she was built, but he had not been prepared for the luscious bounty he unearthed. Full, rosy nipples puckered, begging for his touch, his mouth. Her breasts were bottom heavy, rounded, too big for his hands. Without the ability to wait, to coax, he leaned down and took a nipple fully into his mouth. She moaned his name and speared her hands through his hair. She shifted against him, restless. She tempted him to rush as she slid one hand down his body to his cock. She stroked him through the fabric of his pants, teasing him with the barest of touches.

His cock grew, his balls drew up, and, Lord, he felt a drop of pre-cum ease out. He hadn't even gotten his pants off, and he was ready to come. Wade raised his head and looked down at her. She was already flushed, her body soft and willing, and she had barely had any foreplay.

"You better stop that, or it will be over before I even get us started."

Her full, swollen mouth formed a perfect "O." God, he couldn't wait to ease his shaft between those lips and have her tongue slip over the head. His hands shook at the images swirling in his head. But that would have to wait because tonight he planned on being buried deep in her pussy when he came.

He pulled away and started grasping at her skirt. It didn't take him but a few seconds to slide it down her legs and throw it on the floor behind him. Her damp panties followed a second later.

"Take off your shirt and bra."

She hesitated, and he could understand why. He had never heard his voice so stark with need, and it scared the hell out of him. But there was something about her, something that urged him to take complete possession of not just her body, but also her soul. It went above and beyond simple lust. This was almost primal.

She removed the rest of her clothing, and he kneeled beside her on the bed taking in the entire view. Damn, she was gorgeous. He knew if he told her she would just ignore it, say it was because of the sex, but he meant it. The woman was so giving, so loving, and she had a body that he could only dream of before tonight. Full breasts, rounded hips, and shapely legs. He knew without a doubt she would have them wrapped around him tonight. The surprise of the night was the stockings. They weren't fancy, but they hugged her thighs and became the perfect frame for the golden brown curls at the apex of her thighs. He slipped his hand over them and felt a shock of excitement when his fingers came away wet.

"You said you would be naked, too."

Her voice was just above a whisper, and he could hear the blush in it, but there was something else. The same craving he felt blazing through his blood vibrated in her voice—called to him. He looked up at her face, then slowly, without breaking eye contact, unbuttoned his shirt, slipping it off his shoulders, his pants, shoes, and socks were soon discarded somewhere behind him.

When he covered her with his body, everything in his soul told him to take, to push himself to the hilt and enjoy the wet clasp of her sex. He held back. He wanted this to go further, wanted her to know just how good it could be.

With a smile, he slipped down her body, licking, nibbling and caressing. When he slipped his tongue over her stomach, her muscles quivered. She came up on her elbows and stared down at him.

"Oh, Wade, no."

He chuckled because it was a half-hearted protest. As before, he could hear the desire in her voice. He tore his attention away from her face and looked at her pussy. Her curls were damp with her juices. He drew in a deep breath, enjoying the musky scent of her arousal. His mouth watered with the need to taste her.

The moment he slipped his tongue between her folds, she moaned. The flavor of her, sweet and sassy, exploded across his tongue, dazzled his senses. She lifted herself against his mouth, her moans growing as he thrust his tongue into her hot core again and again. He knew it wouldn't take much to push her over the edge, and he was tempted to do just that. He wanted her so far gone she would not be able to think.

He took her hardened clit into his mouth and sucked. Her moans grew in volume, her legs shifting restlessly beside him. She shuddered as he slipped a finger into her pussy. God, her muscles clamped down so hard on his digit, he felt another drop of cum slip from his cock. Just the thought of what it would feel like as he thrust into her tight, wet passage almost wiped out what little control he had left.

He gathered her juices, eased his finger out and down to her anus. She froze. It told him what he wanted to know, and he could not help but feel smug. No man had ever taken her like that, and Wade couldn't wait to the one who did. He slowly eased his finger in.

"Wade?"

He looked up her body at her face. "Tell me if you don't like it."

"I..." She shivered. Since she seemed at a loss for words, he decided to help out.

"How does it feel? Do you like feeling my finger?" He closed his eyes, and the scene he thought of one too many times came blazing across his mind. He dreamed of bending her over a table and easing into that tight ass of hers. Good Lord, when he drew his hand away, it shook. "Hmm, I can't wait to bend you over and slid my cock into your tight hole."

Her quickly drawn in breath was filled with shock and colored with arousal. Need rode him hard. His cock pulsed, begging for relief.

He slipped his hands under that full, rounded ass and lifted her pussy to his mouth. He made sure she could not move, taking complete control of her. He devoured her now, pushing his way into her pussy, lapping at her juices, sucking and licking her clit. Minutes later, she stilled, then convulsed.

"Oh, Wade. Oh. My. God." She screamed his name again as she came. He looked up at her as a look of pure pleasure washed over her features. His body responded, demanding release.

He rose to his feet and grabbed the condom he'd put on the nightstand. She still shivered from her release as he eased his way into her tight, hot, clinging passage. Her muscles clamped down on him and he stilled. His body quivered, needing relief, but another part of him clenched, warmed. His chest felt the quick, hard kick of lust and love, adding another layer of heat to their joining.

Fuck, this felt so right. The only missing piece of the puzzle was Marc, but Wade brushed that aside. Right now, he wanted to enjoy, to feel her come again, to complete what they had started.

He pulled almost all the way out and plunged back into her again, building her back up to the edge again. With each thrust, he pushed both of them further. He lifted himself to his knees, taking her hips in his hands, and pounded into her again and again.

"Oh, Wade!" She climaxed again, her muscles pulling him deeper and stripping his orgasm from him. He thrust into her to the hilt as his balls drew up tight. He shuddered as he came, hot bliss washing over him as he gave himself over to his release.

Moments later, he collapsed beside her, then pulled her into his arms. India snuggled against him, her curves pressed against him. She sighed, the sound of satisfaction easy to hear. Contentment like he had never known settled in his chest, warming him. Everything felt right, felt just as it should be but for one glaring problem, Marc.

He brushed a soft kiss on her forehead, and she let out a little feminine snore. Smiling, he decided that he would take care of his friend tomorrow. Marc wouldn't know what hit him was the last thought Wade had before drifting off to sleep.

* * * *

India rolled over and felt for Wade. Cold sheets met her palm. Sitting up, she frowned wondering where he could be. She listened for a moment and noted that the house was silent. Wade could move quietly if needed, but she had wooden floors throughout the house. She would have heard him if he were there.

Disappointment dampened what should have been a wonderful morning. Frowning, she grabbed her silk robe. The soft fabric slid over her skin and she sighed. She loved the feel of silk, but this was the only piece of clothing she could afford right now. It was her one indulgence, she thought as she looked down at her toes. She missed pedicures.

She pushed herself from her self-pity and padded barefoot out into the living room–kitchen. When she didn't find Wade there, she felt another twinge of self-pity. He hadn't even woken her up to say goodbye. Odd, given is pursuit of her last night, but then...maybe after his conquest, he got bored. Lord knew he could do better than a thirty-five year old trying to put her life back on track.

With a sigh, she moved to the kitchen table and there, scrawled in strong masculine writing, was a note from Wade.

*Be right back. Don't get dress on my account.*
*W-*

India couldn't stop the giddiness that shifted through her, or the giggle that escaped. Oh, she had it bad if just a little note saying that he was coming back made her this happy. There was no way this was going anywhere. They were just not right for each other. And she had a business to run. But she at least wanted a chance at more great sex.

She closed her eyes remembering the second time they made love. She'd come awake quite suddenly, her body already shivering from the pleasure he created with his hands and his mouth. He mounted her the minute he realized she was truly awake. Even now, she could feel her pussy clench at the memory, a gush of liquid filing her slit.

He'd turned her into a nympho.

A knock sounded at the door. Her heart jumped, her breathing hitched. *He was back.* Without looking, she unlocked and opened it. All her happiness faded when she found Johnny standing on her doorstep, a dozen roses in hand.

# Chapter Five

Wade pulled up behind a BMW and immediately knew something was wrong. One look at India's porch told him that "something" was another man. A twist of jealousy hit him so hard in the chest, he almost growled. What the hell was she doing entertaining a man on her porch? Good Lord, she was wearing some little red number in plain view of another man. He was pretty sure there was nothing beneath it from the outline of her breasts.

Their voices raised and a look of fear passed over India's face. Without thinking, he was out of his truck and striding up the walk.

He stopped short of grabbing the man by the collar and throwing him to the curb.

"I just want to talk about you coming back to work for our company." The man whined like a little boy, and it was at that point that Wade realized this must be the ex-husband.

"India has her own business now."

The man whirled around, his movements so overblown, it was almost comical. When India looked up at him, relief softened her features. It warmed his heart the way she looked at him, as if he were exactly what she needed.

"Who the hell are you?"

The ex's question brought Wade's attention back to him and he frowned. He thought he would be older, fatter, and hopefully uglier, but he wasn't. In fact, he looked the picture of health and wealth.

"Wade Thompson. I'm a friend of India's." He offered his hand to shake, but the idiot just kept staring at him as if he were from another planet. Of course, he might be able to tell if Wade touched him. There was a good chance he would hurt the bastard. Wade dropped his hand.

The ex sneered. "A little early to be calling on a friend."

Wade's fingers burned to wrap around the jackass' neck and choke the life out of him. One look at India had him pausing. Any altercation would cause a scene, and he knew India wouldn't be happy.

"I'm returning."

The man's eyes widened then narrowed. "What the hell does that mean?"

"It means I spent the night here, and while I don't mind India having male friends, I truly don't like having them pop up at six in the morning."

With an aggravated huff, her ex turned to face India. "Did you spend the night with this man?"

Wade had never really seen India mad. She was always so easy going, with a secret smile that made him think she found most of life amusing. Even though it wasn't directed toward him, Wade almost took a step back at the pure rage that flashed over her face and darkened her eyes.

"What right do you have asking me that?"

A smart man would have recognized her anger, would have backed away or apologized. Her ex-husband was not a smart man.

"We're barely divorced and you're fucking anything that comes along?"

He opened his mouth to explain he wasn't just anything, but the look on India's face stopped him. She went from furious to borderline murderous in the blink of an eye. She stepped off her porch and her ex apparently realized just how pissed India was. An angry flush added color to her golden skin. She looked like an Amazon. Damn, he wanted to pick her up, take her into the house, and make love to her all over again.

"Me? Me?! You were the one who decided to fuck my cousin, all the while I built one of the best franchises in Texas. Then, in your wisdom, you dumped me for a woman who was barely legal. What was it that you said?" She paused. The asshole opened his mouth, but he apparently realized just how dangerous India was right now and shut it. "Right. 'Sorry, love, but other than our mutual goal with the restaurants, I really don't need you.' You called me boring. Me!"

"You were always working and you never wanted to go anywhere."

Jesus, he was stupid.

"Yes, I was. While you were flitting off to Vegas and Hawaii and Miami, I was working. I was earning the money. So, if someone was lacking in our relationship, I think it was you. Until I came along, you couldn't earn a dollar. You failed as a provider."

She drew in big gulps of air, and Wade was mesmerized. Damn, he knew the woman had fire in her, but he had no idea it was so damned sexy.

All his admiration turned deadly the minute her ex stepped forward and threw the flowers down. His threatening stance had Wade moving closer.

"You ball-busting bitch. It wasn't my fault you were always so cold in bed. It was like sleeping with a dead woman."

Anger morphed to rage as Wade stepped forward and grabbed the ex by the collar. "This is where you find something else to do."

He dragged the man back to his beamer and tossed him against it. He bounced off it, and Wade shoved him again. "Listen to me, you little bastard. You even think of coming over here again, I'll beat you beyond recognition. They'll have to use dental records to identify your body. Do you understand me?"

All the color drained out of his face as he nodded.

"Now, get back in the car and leave. And pray to God I don't find you somewhere in a dark alley. Do you understand me? I'm restraining myself because I don't want to upset India anymore, but if I find you alone, all bets are off."

Wade pushed himself away from the car, breathing heavily, the need to destroy something pumping through his veins.

He watched the coward trip over himself to get into the car. Once he pulled away from the curb, Wade counted back from ten, trying to calm the need to destroy.

He turned and found India watching him, her face bloodless, all the sexy anger completely drained. His heart ached, his body moved forward with only one thing on his mind, comfort.

He bent to pick up the flowers, but she said, "Leave them. He always used flowers to cover up his lies. They can die there."

No emotion filled her voice, her eyes unfocused on the ground in front of her.

"India, hun?"

She looked up and shivered. Pain twisted his chest. Oh, God, he hoped she wasn't scared of him. "Honey, let's go in."

She nodded and turned to walk in. When he came up the steps, she moved away from him. He didn't want her to fear him, but Wade knew that the blame could be laid at the feet of her ex-husband.

"How about I get some coffee started?"

"I have to get ready. I have a wedding booked today."

Flat, unemotional. This was not like India at all. She was bubbly, happy, always ready with a smile. His worry turned to panic.

"A cup of coffee will get your engines revving."

When she said nothing, Wade walked around to look at her face. The mortification he saw stamped on her features caused another worry.

"India?"

"Could you please just leave?"

The desperation in her voice tore at his heart. "I don't want to leave."

When she finally looked at him, her eyes shimmered with unshed tears. He gulped, trying to rid himself of the knot in his throat.

"I can't deal with this."

"He's gone. He won't be back."

She blinked and the tears trickled down her face. "I can't deal with you, with all of this. Don't you understand?" The last of it came out on a sob.

He reached for her and she backed away. Something in his chest twisted.

"I'll ruin it. What the hell was I thinking? I couldn't keep him happy. How would I keep a man like you happy?"

Slowly, as if she were an animal he might spook, he slid his hand into hers, then up her arm.

"I don't know what your marriage was like, but it sounds like your ex was a pretty self-absorbed prick."

She laughed, although there was no joy in it. "I mistook it for confidence. Little did I know the only way he could feel confident was screwing someone younger, someone who never questioned his authority."

"Sounds like you were lucky to get away from him."

She looked at him now. "Yeah. I could have done without the cheating and ruining a business I built. I didn't think he'd come by again, but I know things are desperate."

"He's been by before."

She nodded. "A few weeks ago...the night I had dinner with you and Marc."

The first day they met. "But you haven't had any other problems with someone breaking into your house?"

She shook her head. "He wouldn't do that again."

Anger had his blood heating again. When he spoke, his voice was deadly soft, but India seemed not to notice. "He's done it before? Broke into your house?"

"Do we really have to get into this?"

Crossing his arms over his chest, Wade stared at her.

She rolled her eyes and walked over to the coffee pot. "Johnny really didn't understand what divorcing me meant. Especially when he went after the business."

She filled up the coffeemaker then motioned to the table. He didn't want to sit down like they were having some goddamn casual conversation. She had an ex-husband who had broken into her house, and she was acting as if it was no big deal.

Once they were settled at the table, she continued."See, Bunny—"

"Bunny?"

She sighed. "My cousin Bunny isn't the brightest bulb. But when your daddy is Nelson Delgado, it doesn't really matter. So, she latched on to Johnny, not realizing that Johnny has no business sense. I was behind our success. Yes, Johnny had the contacts, but he also has a horrific temper. I spent a lot of my time smoothing over problems he created."

Fury whipped through him, and he grabbed her wrist. She looked down at his hand then raised her gaze to him. One eyebrow rose in question.

"You're telling me that your ex has a temper and he broke into your house?"

She sighed again. "I have a restraining order."

He snorted. "A fat lot of good that will do. He can just walk up to you anytime."

She nodded. "I agree. But with each incident, I call the police. He's building up a nice little portfolio with the San Antonio Police Department."

He released her wrist. "I don't know if I like you staying here by yourself."

She blinked. "What?"

"It isn't safe for you here." Rage and helplessness had him by the balls. Johnny wasn't a prize, but he was in good shape, and it wouldn't take anything for the man to break into her house. She wouldn't have a chance against the bastard.

"I think I know what's good for me, and I have no problem being here on my own."

He could tell he stepped over some invisible line by the tone in her voice. And dammit, that made him angrier. He wanted the right to step over the line, to protect her and keep her safe. His primal beast roared to life, trying to take control. Wade punched him back down. That day would come, but he didn't have that right...not yet.

"I'm sorry." He took her hand and pulled her out of the chair and into his arms. She was warm and soft, her luscious breasts pressed against his chest. Just touching her had his cock twitching, his heart racing.

"I didn't mean to sound like I was telling you what to do. I just...I can't stand for a woman to be put in a situation like that."

She looked up at him. "Just so you know, you can't order me around. I gave that up the day I signed my divorce papers."

He frowned. "Now I understand that you might not like me telling you what to do in your life." He slid his hand down to her full ass. "But I take exception to certain areas of your life."

She smiled, her lips curving into a sultry invitation.

"And just where do you think you should be able to boss me around?"

He lifted his hand and slapped her ass. She gasped, the sound filled with excitement and surprise had his blood churning, cock hardening.

"I think you need a lesson in submission."

* * * *

Horror and arousal shot through India's blood. She didn't like dominant men, didn't like being told what to do and when to do it. What she told Wade was true. She didn't want any person telling her what to do in her personal or professional life. But somewhere deep inside her, she was thrilled at the hot, dark look in his eyes as she untangled herself from his arms.

She took a step back, her heart jerking when he followed. She almost tripped over her chair, then rounded it holding it in front of herself. His lips curved.

"Are you going to make me chase you?"

Her first thought was no way. She didn't get into parlor games when it came to sex. Apparently, since she didn't answer, Wade took that as a yes and lunged for her. With a squeal, she shot off, running around the table and into her living room. There wasn't much room in her small house, but she knew how to get around more readily than Wade. She ran around her coffee table, and he had her cornered by the easy chair. She faked a move to the right. Wade was too fast when she moved to her left. He tackled her, causing both of them to fall over onto the couch.

She laughed as he stretched his length out on top of her. "Woman, you make me chase you even after I've had you."

She frowned. "You didn't chase me."

He laughed, his chest vibrating against her breasts. "You have led me on a merry chase. All those lunches, those long looks. I'm damn proud of myself for behaving as long as I did."

"Why did you?"

He laughed again. "I couldn't seduce someone we just hired. Plus, this was more fun. Now put her hands over your head."

She didn't respond.

"Don't make me take you over my knee. I'll make that ass of yours red."

A hot thrill shot through her, a gush of arousal wetting her sex. Oh, this was bad. He was threatening to punish her, and she was getting off on it. He had really turned her into a nympho. She slowly lifted her arms. With easy movements, he slid the tie from her robe and wrapped it loosely around her wrists.

He offered her one of his naughty smiles as he pulled the robe open. The moment his mouth touched the sensitive skin between her breasts, she melted. The man had one of the most talented mouths.

"I'm definitely going to enjoy this lesson," he said, his voice rough with desire. She knew it would probably be better for her if she stopped him. India knew there was no chance for the two of them, but as he slipped down her body, using that talented mouth on her flesh, she pushed aside the worry.

His tongue moved over her nipple, first circling the tip, then pulling the entire nipple into his mouth. As he teased one with his mouth, he rolled the other between two of his fingers, then pinched. The bite of pleasure-pain moved through her swiftly, sending a jolt of heat to her blood. She wanted to touch, needed to, but could not get her hands free.

She growled in frustration. Wade shot her a knowing smile but said nothing as he blew on her wet nipple. She shivered. He did not break eye contact as he moved to her other breast and took the turgid tip into his mouth. The air backed up in her lungs as he teased her, his tongue lapping over the nipple, his teeth grazing the very tip.

"Wade."

He pulled away and frowned up at her. "I think I told you I was in charge."

She opened her mouth to argue with him, but he placed his hand over her lips.

"Uh, uh, uh." He tweaked her nipple and she moaned. "I said I was in charge. If you're bad, there will be spanking involved."

A flush of heat warmed her chest, then crawled up into her face.

He laughed. "I think I just found something else you might like, but that will have to wait."

Before she could say anything, he pressed his mouth between her breasts, then moved down her torso. Nips, the flash of tongue, all of it sent her senses into overdrive. He wasn't rushing, he wasn't even being pushy. He methodically moved down her body, teasing, caressing her with his mouth. When he reached her mound, he placed a kiss at the very top of it, then nipped. Desire sparked then shivered over her nerve endings. The next instant, his mouth was on her, his tongue slipping between her dripping folds. Not enough to push her over, just enough to make her tense, edgy, and ready to beg for relief. He pushed one finger into her as he continued his delicious assault, but even that was a tease. He did everything he could to avoid her clit.

She was ready to scream when he slowly pulled her finger out of her pussy, gathering her juices, and then slipped it down to her ass. She instantly tensed, but he ignored her, first teasing the hole, then slowly pushing inside. Instantly, she felt full, the strange feeling a strange mixture of pleasure and pain that had her craving for more.

"Easy, darlin'." His voice was smooth, comforting. "You have to get used to this."

She wanted to ask why, but she couldn't seem to find the words. He placed his mouth on her clit, licking, nipping at it, edging her closer to climax. The exquisite torture drove her out of her mind. If she thought about it, she would be ashamed, enjoying something so forbidden, but at the moment, the amazing sensual haze he was creating didn't allow for that. Excitement had her body racing to the finish, begging for the relief she knew only he could give her. When she thought it wouldn't happen, that she would be tortured forever, he rolled her clit into his mouth, his teeth grazing over it. In the next instant, she fell into a morass of pleasure. All the tension he built exploded.

"Wade!" She thrashed, her body shaking violently from her climax. She wasn't even done before he pulled his finger out then plunged in again, his tongue thrusting between her folds, and she was coming again.

She was still recovering when he moved away from her. She heard him cuss and lazily opened her eyes. He had undone his pants and fumbled with a condom. When she saw his desperate need etched on his facial features, she could only stare in wonder. She caused this.

Before she could revel in that, he pulled her up and off the couch, sitting down and then placing her on his lap. She slipped her still tied hands over his head. With little finesse, he lifted her up and plunged into her core.

Her swollen sex gripped him, pulled him deep within in her. Instead of the frenzied movements she expected, he moved slowly. She looked down at him and found him watching her, heat burning in his eyes, his expression so intense, so passionate, tears filled her eyes. Everything she had felt for her ex slipped away, and she lost herself in this man, the one who made her feel special, sexy…needed.

His fingers dug into her flesh as she started to increase the rhythm. When she paid him no heed, he smacked her ass. The sting of his palm sent a shockwave of thrilling heat from that point. She smiled at him, knowing she was pushing him closer, reveling in the power she felt over him.

"India."

She ignored the warning in his voice and leaned down to brush her mouth over his. The moment she slipped her tongue between his lips, she closed her eyes. The pungent taste of her own arousal danced over her tongue. Arousal built, but this time, it was more acute…almost brutal. Everything he had given her, from friendship to the night before, came rushing back to her. No man had ever made her feel so wanted, so sexy, so craved. Her chest tightened with an emotion she couldn't seem to interpret…probably would never be able to. But she knew that wasn't important. What was important was his pleasure. She needed to do this more than she needed to breathe.

She pulled away, her vision now blurry with the tears, but she watched him. Her own arousal spiked as she watched his eyes darken. His shout as he came pushed her over the edge, ripping another orgasm from her soul. Waves of ecstasy pummeled her, washed over her, drained her. She collapsed against his chest as he wrapped his arms around her.

Warmth filled her, surrounded her even when she felt a little crack in her heart. For Wade, this would be enough, but she knew now that she would never get over him. He never promised more, and she would not fault him when he left.

She would just try her best to enjoy the ride. It was the only thing that would make the heartbreak worth it.

# Chapter Six

The moment Marc heard the door open, he took a deep breath and released it. Frustration had been his companion the last few hours of a long night, and he didn't need to take it out on Wade—even if he was the reason for it. Or rather, where Wade had been.

"About time you got home."

Marc winced at the irritation he heard in his voice. When he looked up, Marc knew from the lazy satisfaction on Wade's face where his friend had been and with whom. Of course, there had been little doubt he would succeed.

"I told you what I was doing last night. Did you think I was lying?"

Marc shook his head knowing that Wade never changed his mind once it was set. Unfortunately, he worried that Wade would get his heart ripped out in the process. He'd been there with Michelle.

"What the hell do you think you're doing?" he asked.

"Right now, I'm going to take a quick shower and get dressed for a wedding."

Marc's heart jerked, and he felt his face drain of blood.

Wade chuckled. "Oh, man, you should see your face."

Anger and frustration had Marc on his feet and moving toward Wade. "What the hell are you talking about?"

"Calm down. I'm not making a trip to Vegas, *yet*." He crossed his arms over his chest. "India's catering a wedding reception. I'm tagging along."

"So you're going through with this?"

"*We* are, as soon as you pull your head out of your ass. And besides, I don't want to leave her alone. Her ex showed up this morning. She apparently has a restraining order against him."

Everything in Marc stilled, the cold fury whipped through him. "What did he do?"

"Nothing, except break into her house before. That's why she had the restraining order. She stood up to him and man, oh man, don't ever make her mad. She lit into him pretty bad." He wiggled his eyebrows. "Pretty damned sexy when she's mad—especially since she was only wearing a red silk robe."

Wade closed his eyes and hummed. Marc curled his fingers into the palms of his hands to keep from strangling him.

"Focus, Wade. What happened with the ex?"

Wade opened his eyes, and now they were dark with rage. "Bastard was trying to get her back with roses. Do you know that he cheated on her…with her cousin?"

Marc suspected it from a few things she said. "Did he threaten her?"

Wade shook his head. "But I could read it. I felt it down to my bones he wanted to hurt her."

Marc didn't question that. Wade had seen the worst part of life in the foster homes he'd grown up in. Before being tossed into the system, Wade's home life had been just as bad. His own father had been an angry, bitter man who took all of his frustrations out on his wife. Wade had suffered at that bastard's hands. His friend knew exactly what it felt like to be abused by a person who should be there to love and protect him.

"Did you set him straight?"

Wade sneered. "Yeah. Bastard probably pissed in his pants."

"How did India take it?"

Wade's expression softened. "At first, she was a bit upset. The man actually had the nerve to say she was a dead fish in bed. Like she could be. That woman is a firecracker, let me tell you."

Just hearing the satisfaction in Wade's voice had Marc's blood humming. Jesus, he needed to get laid. He had a few ladies toss out some signals at their party, but he hadn't been tempted, even just to release his pent up need. None of them had been India.

"Do you have the guy's name?"

Wade nodded. "Johnny Anderson."

"I'll look him up. I'm sure I can bend a few arms and get the police report."

"Police reports. India keeps reporting every interaction."

Impotent rage flashed through his blood. "Those are useless."

"That's why I plan on staying as close as possible."

He headed off to his room leaving Marc alone with his thoughts. *Goddamn him.* If Wade hadn't touched her, Marc would be okay. Oh, he'd still lust after her, but he could keep it at bay. Now that Wade had been with her…

Marc closed his eyes. He could just imagine how she responded. The few times they talked in the last few weeks told Marc that she was sweet and sensual. The type of woman who had no idea she was sexy as hell. Being the person who showed her just how sensual she was would be a dream come true. He opened his eyes and looked out over the Riverwalk. He turned the idea over in his mind.

Since Michelle, he hadn't wanted to even think about trying another serious relationship. When she made him choose between her and Wade, Marc walked away. Definitely not with his heart whole. But he had known that if Michelle understood him and truly loved him, she would have never asked for that. He'd been shattered.

With India…she had such a giving nature, a personality that told him she would be more than happy to nurture a man. That was one of the reasons he knew Wade was attracted to her. Hell, it was one the reasons he was attracted, also. Who wouldn't want a woman who was like that? Wade and Marc hadn't lived a cushy life while in the Marines, and having someone there to comfort he could count on was more than he had hoped for.

Marc shook his head. He wanted India, knew that it would be damned near impossible not to get involved with her. But he had to at least try. He couldn't go through the pain again. Michelle might have been a grade-A bitch, but she had also done him a favor. There could be no forever in a relationship with three people.

\* \* \* \*

India sighed as she parked in front of her house. It had been one long day. From Johnny showing up, to dealing with a bride from hell—who also had the mother from hell—it hadn't been easy. Her feet and back ached. She just wanted to collapse in bed and not wake up for a week.

A bright light filled her car. She glanced up in her mirror and couldn't help but smile. Wade followed her home again, worried Johnny would show up. No matter how many times she told him not to bother, Wade refused to listen. It went against her feminist side, the one that wanted to stand on her own, but she had to admit she felt a little safer with Wade around.

She gathered her purse and stepped out of her car. Before she could straighten and shut the door, Wade was there beside her.

"Who was that scary lady you were talking to?" Wade asked, taking her key and locking her car door for her.

She laughed because that described Marilyn Graves to a T. "Mother of the bride. I'll screen my calls for them again. The money just isn't worth it."

"What was she so mad about?"

India opened her mouth to explain but stopped when she noticed her front window had been shattered. Her lace curtains blew through the jagged, broken glass. An icy shiver slipped down her spine.

"What's the matter?"

She nodded to her porch. "The window."

Wade frowned and moved closer to the house. When he cursed, she knew he'd finally seen it. He wrapped his hand around her upper arm and walked her to his pickup.

"Get in."

The low, deep growl sent a quiver to her tummy. It was so unlike the Wade she knew. Easygoing Wade, even seductive Wade, never used that tone.

Once she was seated, he said, "Call 911. Then call Marc on his cell."

"I don't have Marc's cell number," she said as she called the police.

"Never mind, I'll call him. Just get the police here, *now*."

He opened the glove box and pulled out a gun. Another slice of fear shifted through her. Before she could say anything, he slammed the door shut. As she gave operator details, Wade stalked up to her house, his every move controlled. He stepped up onto the porch, and even from a distance, she knew if anyone were in the house, they did not hear him.

Wade slipped into through the front door. Her breath caught in her throat as time suspended. Her pulse hammered out of control until Wade came out and strode down the walk toward her. He pulled out his phone, and she assumed he was calling Marc.

He turned his back to her. With the window up, she could only hear a few words. From the rigid set of his shoulders, she could tell he was still on alert. When he turned back around, his grim features told her she hadn't seen the worst of it.

She opened the door, but he stepped forward and refused to let her out of the pickup. Even as she felt anger pouring off him in waves, his touch was gentle.

"No, it's best that we wait here."

She frowned. "But you went in."

"I wanted to make sure the bastard had left. Better we don't touch anything inside." His voice held no warmth and she shivered.

"Did they take anything?" She had renters insurance, but she truly didn't want to replace things. It would take her forever to deal with insurance.

"Not that I can tell."

His cold manner was as it should be. She understood security was his profession, but she didn't care. She didn't want half answers and cold behavior. Dammit, she needed reassurances and hugs.

Lord, now she sounded like some little girl. She couldn't help it. The idea that someone had broken into her house and messed with her things sent a shard of ice threading through her blood. Johnny hadn't broken in last time. He just had the landlord let him in. Her new landlord wouldn't allow for it.

"Do you think it was Johnny?"

The quiet fury she saw leap into his eyes gave her the answer she needed, but she still needed to hear it from him.

"Yes."

Sirens sounded in the distance, heralding the arrival of the police. She thanked the 911 operator, hung up, and she breathed a sigh of relief.

A young officer stepped out of his car and headed over in their direction as another one approached the house.

"Sir. Ma'am, are you India Singer?"

She nodded.

"I'm Officer Franklin. Can you tell me what happened?"

"I had a wedding I catered this afternoon and evening. Everything was locked up tight when I left."

One eyebrow raised in question. "Are you sure?"

Anger lit her blood, but she banked it. "Yeah, I'm pretty sure because he wouldn't have had to bash in my window."

His cheeks pinkened and she felt a little guilty. He was young, but she just didn't have the patience to go through such asinine questioning.

She opened her mouth. Wade beat her to it. "You want to check out Johnny Anderson. He was here this morning, left angry. India has a restraining order against him."

Speculation darkened the young officer's eyes. The other officer was on his radio calling another unit, then he approached them, his lips in a straight line.

"I called CSI."

The other officer looked surprised. "There isn't any—"

"No, but he did enough damage to call them in."

"Ms. Singer, this is Officer Daniels."

India tried to smile at the other man, but the tension in the air vibrated with testosterone. She went through some more questioning, asking who knew she lived there, what kind of problems she had with Johnny in the past. The CSI unit showed up, and the officers poured out of the van.

Wade looked at her. "Will you be all right by yourself?"

She snorted. "I'm surrounded by San Antonio's finest. I'll be okay."

He hesitated. Another car came tearing around the curb. "About time."

When Marc unfolded his length from the sporty little car, India could not have been more surprised. He strode over, his face an ice sculpture. Great, just what she needed, another man walking around ready to do violence, but no one there to take it out on.

He didn't even look at Wade. He focused his clear eyes on her, concern easily read. "You didn't get hurt?"

She started to shake her head and found herself pulled out of the cab into a bear hug. His massive arms enclosed her in warmth, killing the chill that had been sitting in her blood since she saw the window. She shivered and relaxed into his heat.

"I'll see what the officers are up to," Wade said leaving them alone.

As if Wade's voice brought him out of some kind of trance, Marc eased away, apology in his expression.

"I'm sorry. I didn't mean to manhandle you."

Tears filled her eyes. "No, it actually felt good. I've been trying, trying..."

She hiccupped and the dam broke as fresh tears started to fill her eyes. The fright she had been holding at bay came crashing down on her head, and she started to shake. He pulled her back into his arms, and she curled closer, needing his warmth.

His gentle strokes down her spine calmed her sobs. "I'm sorry."

"For what? Getting upset your ex broke into your house? You have every right to."

She shook her head. "No, really, I didn't mean to slobber on you."

She tried to pull away, but he held her tighter.

"I like you slobbering on me. Besides, you can be upset for both of us. The thought of you showing up earlier...and if Wade hadn't been here."

He shuddered. Anger and fear rolled off him. *For her?* They had struck up a friendship through their phone conversations, but she hadn't realized the depth of his feelings. Greedy for comfort, she burrowed closer, allowing his body heat to surround her. She drew in a deep breath and with it, his scent. Bay rum with a dash of Marc.

Moments later, she pulled away, fell back onto the seat, and looked up at him. He cupped her face and slipped his fingers over his cheeks, wiping away her drying tears.

"I don't even want to think about what could have happened to you."

India did not doubt his sincerity. It vibrated in his voice. But there was something else, something that told her that this was more than just a friend worrying about a friend. And, oh, God, her body reacted to him. Her stomach clenched, her blood warmed. Embarrassed, she closed her eyes.

"Don't."

She opened her eyes. "Don't what?"

"Don't worry about that."

How could he know what she was thinking? That she was desperately trying not to fall in love with both of them, but she couldn't. While she enjoyed Wade and craved his lightness of spirit, she also ached for Marc. So sure and steady, and both of them were driving her mad. How could two men she barely knew affect her this way?

"We'll talk about it later."

At that moment, Wade came forward, her overnight bag in his hand.

She frowned. "What's that for?"

"I thought you could go home with Marc."

"But the police—"

"Have told me that they have what they need for now. They'll come by the apartment tomorrow if they have any other questions."

"I have to go through, make sure nothing was taken."

"You can do that tomorrow, but I don't think he took anything. That wasn't his aim."

He handed the bag to Marc without any agreement from her.

"Wait a minute. I haven't said I'd stay with you. I can easily call my friend Delilah and spend the night with her." That was if Delilah didn't have company—which she usually did on a Saturday night.

Wade gave her a knowing look. "I didn't ask."

Immediately, her body warmed, her nipples hardened. Johnny had broken into her house, and she was being manhandled by a man—a younger man at that—and she was turned on.

Dammit, Wade *had* turned her into a nympho.

Marc took her arm and helped her out of the truck. She turned toward her car, but he tugged her in the opposite direction.

She looked down at the hand wrapped around her arm, then up at Marc. "I'm not leaving my car."

He glanced over it, his expression not giving away his thoughts, but when he looked at her, she was amazed to find amusement lighting his eyes.

"Listen, it might be a piece of crap, but it's my piece of crap. If Johnny shows up here again, there is a good chance he will do something to it."

Marc sighed. "Okay. I'll follow you."

With a roll of the eyes, she wiggled out of his grasp and headed to her car. She said nothing else as she slipped into her seat. She went to close her door, but Wade stepped up. Bracing an arm on the body of the vehicle, he held the other one with his hand.

When he leaned down, she saw the concern in his gaze. "Be careful and don't let Marc rile you...at least until I get home."

Before she could respond to his comment, he gave her a quick, hard kiss, then slammed the door in her face. Just that little touch, not exactly sensual, and she was trembling. The man had her hot from a kiss that lasted less than five seconds. She had to be crazy going to his apartment. India knew she was in dangerous territory. The rational side of her brain was screaming to run in the opposite direction. But another part of her wanted this, craved to have a crazy fling with a hot hunk of a man. A younger hot hunk of a man.

Brights flashed in her mirror and she looked up. Marc sat in his car behind her, waiting. Another little tendril of heat sped through her blood leaving her almost dizzy with the brutality of it. She was definitely going mental. She pulled away from the curb, and reminded herself neither man had said they would share her.

Just thinking about that, about the pleasure both of them could bring her, had every drop of moisture in her mouth evaporating. Her whole body tingled, and lust danced over her nerve endings. She tightened her hands on the wheel, her knuckles white. She knew if they weren't there, they would be shaking. The thoughts swirling in her head were too delicious, too insane to even contemplate. Besides, she had no idea if what Wade said was true. Marc had never indicated that he was attracted to her in that way.

The memory of the way he held and comforted her came back to her and she shivered. But if he was, and they asked her, she wasn't too sure she would be able to tell either of them no.

\* \* \* \*

Wade walked back up and talked to Officer Daniels. "Anything?"

He shook his head. "CSI is still working the scene."

"Any word on Anderson?"

The young officer frowned. "We have no proof it's him."

Aggravation sat heavy on Wade's chest. Damn the bastard. He should have seen this one coming. Men like Anderson were cowards. They picked fights with people they knew they could beat, and they did things like defile a house. Granted, Wade hadn't thought Anderson would go this route...but still, Wade should have seen it coming. Just the idea that India could have been at home when he showed up had Wade's blood icing.

"I know it's him. I saw him this morning, saw that look."

The officer gave him a measuring look. "You're the owner of T and J Security?"

He nodded.

"Ex-Marine, right?"

"Son, there's no such thing as an ex-Marine."

The officer smiled then looked back up at the house. "Yeah, from what you said, and what I've been able to gather from the officer Ms. Singer's been in contact with, it sounds like him. The writing on the wall is in red, but it's not blood, definitely paint."

Wade had known that. The smell was still fresh when he walked in. But it had been the word, not the actual paint that upset Wade. They both walked up to the front of the house, and just inside the door, on the wall facing the entrance, Anderson had painted the word "Whore."

# Chapter Seven

Marc pulled into the parking garage of their apartment building. He watched India park her piece of shit car in the visitor slot. Anticipation hummed through his veins, his cock twitched with need. He had known the moment Wade called and told him the situation that India would be coming home with them. There would be no argument from Marc. To think of what that bastard did to her house. He took several bracing breaths trying to calm himself down. India didn't know yet about the things the bastard had written on the walls. But if Marc ever met the coward, he would make him pay for every fucking letter.

A knock on his window had him jumping, and he found India standing there watching him. Oh, great. The big security expert was just surprised by the woman in his protection. But then India twisted him inside out since the moment he met her.

He knew she was confused, but at the moment, that didn't matter. What she needed was comfort and security. They would have to tell her the worst of it, but that could wait.

He stepped out of his car, grabbing her bag as he rose out of his seat. He locked his car and took India by her elbow to the elevator.

"Do you think Wade will be long?"

"He'll want to do something with your windows before he leaves."

He pushed the button for the elevator, and he could feel her study him.

"I could have taken care of it."

Now it was his turn to look at her. "Wade will take care of it."

"That's not the point."

There was a tension in her voice that hadn't been there earlier. He figured some of the shock had started to wear off. He followed her onto the elevator.

"I know you could have taken care of it. Wade understands that, too."

She glanced at him from beneath her lashes. "While I appreciate everything both of you are doing, I just want you to know I don't like being handled."

He said nothing as they reached their floor and she followed him to the apartment. Unlocking the door, he waited for her to step over the threshold before he followed her, then locked the door behind him. He put her bag in their spare bedroom, then led her to the kitchen.

"How about something to eat or drink?"

"How about you tell me what this is all about?"

"What do you mean?"

She sighed. "I can't play games. I'm not good at them. I dated very little before I was married and not since my divorce. I was married for most of my adult years, and Johnny was the only man I slept with before Wade."

She blushed after she announced that. Marc stood their transfixed by the sight of her. The lights of the Riverwalk sparkled behind her, and she looked so delicate...so tempting. The idea that she had only one lover before Wade had every ounce of blood in his brain heading south.

He had to take a step back to keep from lunging for her. "We don't play games, either. And nothing will be discussed without Wade here."

She didn't look happy with that. She turned her back to him, watching the activity down on the Riverwalk.

"How about a bath?"

She shot him a questioning look over her shoulder. He raised his hands in defense.

"I meant alone. It might ease some of the tension of the day, help you relax."

She shrugged, but turned to head to her room. He stayed her with his hand and pointed her to the large bathroom he and Wade shared.

"You should use ours. It has a tub to die for."

* * * *

Pleasure washed over India as she sank below the surface of the hot water. When Marc said the tub was to die for, he wasn't kidding. The oval shaped tub could fit at least three people and was deep enough for her to stand in, but there was a ledge for reclining. It was actually more of a miniature pool in a way.

Water lapped at her chin as she closed her eyes. When India's Traveling Feast started making good money, she was going to get a tub like this. A professional kitchen with a six burner gas stove and two ovens...and this tub. She could care less what was included in the rest of the house.

The warm water drew out some of the tension and helped soothe the sore muscles from two days of hard work. She'd been rewarded with several new contacts, and one of the bridesmaids had already made an appointment next week to book her wedding reception. Things were definitely looking up.

Well, that is if she ignored the fact that her ex-husband broke into her house. It still irritated her that Wade had kept her from seeing the house. She knew something had happened, and the worst of this was not over. When Johnny needed someone to come rescue him, he would not give up. If he owed money to Victor, he didn't have any other choice but to latch on to her again. It made no sense in her mind. She didn't have the cash flow to help him even if she wanted to, which she didn't.

She pushed aside worries about Johnny, of what he had done to his life. She couldn't help him now. She had a new life to get started with. The old India would sit in the tub and worry herself into an ulcer about it. There was nothing she could do, so she might as well lock it away, worry about it tomorrow.

Besides, she had a younger lover, one who shared women with his friend. A sharp jolt of heat lanced through her. It was one of her favorite fantasies, one she read time and time again, but she'd never thought it would come true. But just the thought of being shared, of two mouths exploring her, teasing her...She shivered. Wade had been an extraordinary lover, so attuned to her every need. If Marc were half as good, she would probably die from pleasure.

Even just thinking about being in bed with both of them had her body shimmering with heat. God, what the hell had gotten into her? Most women would be happy with just Wade, but here she was hoping for both of them to take her. Damn, she thought with a laugh, she'd become a greedy nympho.

"Nothing like finding a naked woman in our tub enjoying herself."

* * * *

Wade smiled when India's eyes popped open. Despite everything that happened today, he felt much of the tension drain from his body. Just knowing she was in his home, waiting for him...nothing had ever made him feel this content. Damn, but she made him happy. The damp heat had her hair curling even more. Her skin had a pleasant flush, whether from the warmth of the room or her embarrassment, he didn't know. Either way, the sight of her flushed and naked made him want to gobble her up.

"Wade." Embarrassment colored her voice.

His smile spread as he approached the tub. "What?"

She cleared her throat.

When she said nothing, he sat down on the edge. "Not like I haven't seen ya naked."

"Not in bright overhead lights."

"Ah." He didn't move, wasn't about to budge. Instead, he slipped a finger beneath the surface of the fragrant water and stirred. The ripples spread, causing the water to lap up against her breasts. Her nipples hardened, and Wade couldn't resist slipping his fingers around one and tugging. She shivered.

"Wade." Longing filled her voice and spoke to his soul.

"How are you doing?" Wade tried to keep his voice calm. It wasn't an easy task. From the moment he entered the apartment, he knew things had changed. Marc's actions had told him more than any words would have been able to. He never allowed people in their private bedrooms, especially their bath. It was a clear indication that his feelings on the subject of India had changed.

"Okay. I was just thinking about getting out."

Wade slid his hand to her other breast. "Don't rush on my account."

"Or mine," Marc said.

Wade glanced over his shoulder and found his best friend standing at the entrance of the bath, leaning against the doorjamb. Excitement sizzled through Wade's blood as he thought of their night ahead. When he turned to face India, his heart jerked. The momentary trepidation he saw in her expression worried him. He expected it, planned for it, but he hadn't prepared for how it would make him feel.

She opened her mouth. No sound came out as she looked from him to Marc then back to Wade again.

"I told you that we shared women," Wade said.

She nodded.

Wade had to tamp down on his agitation. He could not rush her. She wasn't a groupie from the bar. India wouldn't go looking for an opportunity like this, as the women before her did.

"Y-you want to share me?" Disbelief, arousal, and fear colored her voice.

Marc walked further into the room. "Wade said he explained it to you."

Wade ignored the accusatory tone Marc used. "I didn't expect it to move so fast, and I definitely didn't want to push you tonight if you weren't ready. You've been through a lot." That was partially a lie. Wade was pretty sure that he would try his damnedest to get her into bed with them. "So, will you let us share you?"

"In bed?"

Wade ordered himself to calm down, but it was difficult. Every instinct told him to pull her out of the water and demand, but he knew better. Even if she did agree, both he and Marc would always wonder if she did it because of what happened earlier that night.

"I thought you understood."

Her Caribbean gaze moved over him, then swung to Marc. "I just...it's just odd."

He opened his mouth, but Marc walked farther into the room. "I know it may seem odd to you, still we enjoy it. And I can ensure you that you will, too."

Her face flushed with embarrassment, but she looked Marc in the eye. "It isn't that I think what you do is strange. Okay, it *is* a little out of my realm."

"You read books about it," Wade said and smiled when she turned an even brighter shade of red.

She shook her head. "Those are fantasies."

His irritation soon turned to panic. She didn't sound convinced, and he had been so sure.

Apparently sensing his worries, Marc said, "We can make those fantasies come true."

She shuddered, causing a ripple through the water. "But..."

Marc approached the other side of the tub and sat on the edge. "Tell us."

She closed her eyes. "I just don't know why you would want me." When she opened her eyes, her gaze was clear and direct. "I'm not fishing for compliments. I just want to know why you would pick an older woman like me. Lord knows you two could probably have your pick of women."

Wade opened his mouth, then closed it when Marc took her hand. "First, I question the sanity of any man who doesn't want you. But, both Wade and I don't always go with convention. Look at what we are proposing with you. And you keep talking as if this is something done to you. It isn't. It is something we share, with you, with each other."

The silence stretched as India stared at Marc. The wait became unbearable, so Wade asked, "Will you let us share you?"

\* \* \* \*

India allowed the silence of the room to stretch as her mind reeled from the conversation. Two men—two very hot men—wanted to take her to bed. It was an uncommon day to find one man to want to take her on a date, but here were two younger, totally fuckable men, and they wanted to pleasure her.

It wasn't disgust unfurling deep in her belly, heating her blood. Fear and excitement melded, causing her palms to grow damp. Even as she worried about her reaction, the thoughts of what they would do to her, with her, sent her hormones into overdrive. The water lapping against her hard nipples was enticing and painful. Her sex pulsed, begging for her to say yes.

India glanced at Wade. Concern passed over his face even as he smiled at her. His worry for her warmed her heart, but when she looked at Marc, she came up against a brick wall. The stoic expression sent a chill of apprehension down her spine at first. Then she noticed his leg moving, and he kept shifting his weight on the edge of the tub. In the short time she'd known Marc, patient and utter calm had always been his trademark. This uncharacteristic behavior made her think that he just might be nervous about the situation.

"Can I ask you one question?"

Both of them nodded.

"Why me?"

"We explained that," Wade said.

"No, you didn't. You just said you wanted to share me." Just saying the words sent another shaft of heat spiraling through her body.

"I think I proved last night—not to mention this morning—how much I want you."

"But..."

Marc pursed his lips in thought. "Not sure if either of us can explain it." He looked at Wade. "Can you?"

Wade shook his head. "I told you, one brush up against you and I wanted you. Marc and I have been doing this for years, and it seems that our attraction and sexual appetites work off each other. It intensifies the experience."

Intensifies? Lordy, she couldn't imagine anything more intense than making love with Wade. She looked from Marc to Wade and then back to Marc. It would be wonderful, she was sure of it. That is if she could keep up with them.

She worried her bottom lip and Wade groaned, "Listen, I can be understanding. I can even be a *sensitive* guy, but Jesus, you have to decide. You're driving me crazy."

Laughter bubbled up at his aggravated tone. India covered her mouth, thinking to spare his feelings. It only caused her to snort. When she met his gaze, humor danced in his eyes.

She swallowed another laugh. "I'm sorry."

"Really? It's hard to tell."

"Quit your whining," Marc said. When she looked at him, he continued with a smile. "He can be a bit impatient."

That smile, along with the warm, understanding look in his eyes, melted her resistance. He might seem a bit forbidding at first, but India detected a soft, gooey side to Marc. She wanted to just slip onto his lap and curl into his body heat. He was dependable, the go-to guy of the two, and she felt a bone deep concern for her and her feelings emanating from him.

"So, what do you say, India?" Wade asked, his Southern accent deepening, slipping beneath her control and pulling it loose from her grip.

She should run in the other direction. Men were a complication she avoided the last eighteen months since her husband had left her—until last night. She didn't need them messing with her goals, expecting her to put her life on hold for them. And here she was faced with two men. She didn't even want to think about the problems that could arise from that, both personally and professionally.

But she couldn't fight the fact that this was the one fantasy she loved to read about, think about. From the time she hit her sexual prime several years ago, she had contemplated what it would be like to be taken by two men at once. Johnny would have gone ballistic if she'd suggested it, but now she could live the fantasy, even if it were for one night.

She closed her eyes, hoping that some shred of sanity would intercede, but nothing came. Instead, visions of the three of them in bed appeared, and she could not shake them free. Even as she tried to wrap her mind around the idea, her body urged her on. When she opened her eyes, she looked at Wade, then Marc. Her sex clenched, her pulse doubled, her breasts ached. Every ounce of moisture evaporated in her mouth as she licked her dry lips. She needed this, wanted this more than she wanted any one man.

With courage she didn't feel, she rose out of the water. She couldn't say anything at first. Her heart was beating so hard, she was amazed it stayed in her chest. Her blood heated, spiraling through her veins.

"India?" Wade asked.

She knew they wouldn't hold it against her if she turned tail and ran. They would even allow her to stay with no strings. But she didn't want that. She deserved this and, dammit, she wanted them. For the second time in her life, she would take exactly what she wanted.

They both rose to stand beside the tub. She smiled first at Marc, then Wade.

"India?" Wade asked again.

"Yes."

# Chapter Eight

Marc wanted to shout as relief poured through him, but he didn't want to scare India away. Now that this finally was about to happen, he wanted nothing to get in the way of the two of them claiming her. At the moment, forming words had become difficult. He was pretty sure there was little to no blood left in his head. And why would there be with the vision standing in front of them.

Water sluiced down over her body, her flesh glistening, her nipples erect. His cock hardened, lengthened. Damn, she was sexy. She stood before them with her chin raised, her shoulders back, but he sensed her apprehension. Her show of bravery made her even more enticing.

Wade grabbed one of their oversized towels and walked around to stand beside him. Marc offered her a hand to help her from the tub. Once she stood on the mat, Wade moved in, rubbing the soft towel over her breasts, then down to her sex.

Marc moved in behind her, pressing his penis against her rounded ass. He'd thought they'd need to ease her into it, take it slowly, but the moment he touched her, she moaned, tipping her head back onto his shoulder. The scent of her surrounded him, sweet magnolia…with a dash of cinnamon. Sweetness and spice in one delectable package.

Wade tossed the towel and moved in. He pressed kisses against the column of her throat as Marc moved his hands to her breasts. Her nipples bit into his palms. Wade kissed his way to her mouth and took hers in a hot, hungry kiss. Seeing the way she responded, enjoying her moans and mewls, he could feel a drop of pre-cum wet the head of his cock. He wanted her just like this, between them, screaming with pleasure.

Wade drew away from her, and she moaned in complaint. The men shared a smile, but there was no need to communicate verbally. Marc could read Wade's intention in his eyes. Hell, he could feel it shimmering on the air.

They both took one of her hands and led her into Marc's bedroom, to the king-sized bed that sat in the middle of the room.

"This is your last chance, India. We would never force you to do something, but if you have doubts, now is the time to voice them," Marc said.

She pulled her hands from theirs, then placed a hand on Marc's cheek, then Wade's. "I don't think I could stop now."

Marc turned his head and kissed her hand, moving his mouth over her palm. She shivered when his tongue darted out.

Wade tugged on her hand and motioned her to sit down. They both moved in, but she shook her head.

"I think you both have too many clothes on." She said it with a brave face, but there was a quiver in his voice that told Marc it had taken a lot of courage for her to say it.

Marc looked over at Wade and shared a smile. They both started to undress. Their neediness had them pulling clothes off left and right, and in less than two minutes, they were both naked.

Marc looked at India who wasn't exactly looking at their faces. Her attention was on his cock, and she licked her lips.

He groaned and she looked up at him, and mischievous glint lighting her eyes. Just that satisfied expression, the idea that she knew she could cause him to lose control, had his hands shaking.

Wade got on his knees in front of her and spread her legs. Marc, needing to connect, needing to feel her mouth on his cock, moved to the bed and kneeled beside her.

"Lay down, India." Wade bit out every word, and Marc glanced at him. There was little that could get under Wade's skin, but India did.

Marc had known that from the start. But now he knew the extent for Wade...and for himself. This woman wasn't some groupie who would walk away after their night together, and because of that, they had to make this special, let her know just how special she was to them. It had them both on the emotional edge.

She did as Wade ordered, and he spread her thighs, dipping his head between her legs. India's eyes glazed then closed the moment Wade's mouth touched her. Marc wrapped his hand around his cock and pumped it a few times. Jesus, his balls tightened, and a drop formed on the head of his penis.

Excitement sizzled, the tension growing in the air around the three of them.

"India," Marc said, and waited for her to open her eyes. "I need your mouth on me."

He knew his voice was filled with desperate need, but Marc didn't care. He'd been fantasizing about her for weeks, driving himself crazy on what it would feel like, and now he had to know...needed to know.

She opened her mouth, and he slid his cock between her lips. She levered herself so she could wrap her hand around the base of his penis, and then moved in rhythm with her mouth. Each time she drew up, her tongue swiped over the crown. With each thrust into her warm, wet mouth, he lost a little more control.

Marc didn't know how long he would last, especially when she slipped her hand to his balls and caressed him. Marc looked down at Wade and watched as he slipped one finger into her pussy. Her moans vibrated over his cock, down to his balls, and he had to force himself not to come. He pulled away, trying to gain some bit of control. She smiled up at him as she slid her tongue over her plump lips. The look of satisfaction she gave him told Marc she knew exactly how close he was. He reached down with his hand and squeezed first one, then the other nipple. He was rewarded with a long, throaty moan. Marc bent his head and grazed his teeth over one nipple as he continued to tease the other. It was her turn to shift and moan. And as satisfied as he was for driving her crazy, those little mewls and sighs were driving his arousal higher.

"Christ." Wade pulled away.

When Marc saw the expression on Wade's face, he knew what he wanted, what both of them needed.

"India?"

Her eyes were barely opened, but Marc could read the excitement shimmering there.

"Do you think you could take both of us?"

* * * *

India opened her eyes further and looked up at Marc, then down at Wade as he slipped his hand over her mound. Just the soft caress had her pussy clenching, her body yearning. She wanted this, had fantasized about it more than once, but fear held her immobile. She had never done this before, never allowed a man to take her in such a way. But the looks on their faces, the need she saw mirrored in their eyes, had her throwing her inhibitions away. She refused to deny herself pleasure.

"Yes. Please."

Wade chuckled as he rose and then moved around the bed to the nightstand. She tried to see what was happening, but Marc was there covering her body with his. He held her face in his hands, and without closing his eyes, he bent his head and took her mouth. His tongue slipped in immediately, dancing along hers, tempting, teasing, driving her out of her mind. She wanted to close her eyes, ignore the intensity she saw in Marc's clear gaze, but she could not.

He slipped his hands up and speared his fingers through her hair as he slanted his mouth, closed his eyes, and took the kiss to another level.

Every alarm bell in her body went off. Not in fear, but in pleasure. Damn, the man could kiss, could drive her insane with just his tongue.

India slipped her hands up over his shoulders, trying to pull him closer. The pulse of need that both Marc and Wade built in her morphed into something she could not seem to comprehend or control. It throbbed from her pussy and sent warmth flowing throughout her body. The craving they created took over every other thought.

He rolled them on the bed so that she was on top of him. She gasped. She couldn't help it when she found herself looking down at him. His cock pulsed against her sex. Closing her eyes, she twisted her hips and felt another coating of her juices on her slit.

Wade gained the bed and moved behind her. Marc slid his hands up her torso to her breasts, playing with her nipples, caressing her flesh possessively.

"God, these are gorgeous." Marc weighed them in his hands, then pinched her nipples again.

Wade leaned over her, kissed her neck, then looked down at Marc. "And so fucking responsive. Look at those pretty nipples begging to be touched."

The dark need in both their voices spoke to her own, to an inner appetite she didn't know she possessed. But it swamped her, rising up and taking over any fear she might have had.

Wade moved away, then she felt his finger at her puckered hole. When he first slipped it in, she teared up at the shock of pain. She felt the cool gel he coated his finger with as he pushed past the ring of muscles and slipped all the way in.

"Christ," he said, his voice barely a whisper and filled with awe.

He added another finger coated with gel, and she shuddered as the pleasure-pain twisted through her. Marc slipped his finger over her clit, massaging it, reminding her of what was to come. Both men continued to tease her as the tension in her stomach dropped to her sex. Little shivers of delight moved over her as the men penetrated both holes.

"I can't wait," Marc said.

India opened her eyes at the desperation she heard in his voice. In the weeks she had known him, she had come to think of him as the one in command, but at the moment, he had little of that. He reached beside him where Wade had put two condoms.

With dexterity and amazing speed, he ripped open the condom. She tried to help him put it on, but he pushed her hands away. She giggled at his frown and he looked up.

"You look so cute when you frown," she said then gasped when Wade twisted his fingers inside her anus. Tendrils of pleasure floated through her body and she moaned.

"Don't get so naughty, India," Wade said.

Marc smiled up at her. "We know just how to drive you insane before we give you satisfaction. We'll make you beg."

She opened her mouth to tell him she could handle both of them, but Wade pulled his fingers free as Marc lifted her up. In one hard thrust, he impaled her on his penis. Her inner muscles quivered as they stretched to accommodate his size. God, she felt so full, so overwhelmed.

"Damn, I can feel her muscles tug on my cock. All these little ripples," Marc said.

Holding her hips, he moved her up and down, controlling the depth and speed of his thrusts. She could feel her orgasm building, her body ready to move to that next level, but he kept it out of reach with his slow movements. When he stopped, she moaned. She felt another cool shock of gel in her anus, then Wade's cock poked at her puckered hole.

"India."

She looked down at Marc, at his serious expression. "I want this."

He let out a sigh of pleasure as he moved his hands to her cheeks and pulled them apart for an easier entrance for Wade. Slowly, Wade penetrated. Pain and pleasure entwined as he worked his way in. She flinched as Wade pushed past the tight ring of muscles. Her eyes started to tear up from the shock of pain.

"It's okay, baby. Just relax," Marc said. Gently, he stroked her face, giving her soft kisses.

As Wade sunk deeper, both men groaned. The jolt of it and initial pain faded. Both men seemed to be holding their breaths, waiting for her. She had never felt so incredibly full, as if ready to burst.

Marc cradled her face in his hands again and brushed his mouth over hers. "Nothing but pleasure now. Tell us if it gets to be too much."

She could not speak, dared not to. The look on his face, the need that shimmered in his voice, had her heart twisting. Wade kissed the back of her neck, his mouth and tongue moving over her heated flesh. The pain receded, pleasure taking hold as they thrust in and out of her, working in a rhythm that drove her crazy. As they pushed her to her limits, she lost track of time, her muscles tightening as satisfaction seemed just an inch away. But they gave her no relief.

"Jesus, you feel good," Wade said.

Her orgasm built as they continued their assault. "God, please."

Marc took her mouth in a heated, wet kiss. "What do you want, India? Tell us what you need."

Before she could answer him, her orgasm slammed through her. She convulsed, tightening around their cocks, pulling them deeper into her. Their movements turned frantic, both of them pumping into her. Another orgasm hit her as both men groaned her name.

Long minutes later, she was awakened from a slight doze by Wade as he pulled out of her. Marc lifted her and placed her between them. She felt drained, but at the same time, complete. She snuggled closer to Marc, then reached behind her back for Wade.

Nothing felt quite as wonderful as being between them, their body heat warming her. It was the last thought she had as she drifted into the contented sleep.

# Chapter Nine

Wade woke, his dick hard, his senses on alert. A soft hand cupped his cock, fingers dancing over the tip. He looked down and found India smiling up at him. His heart twisted in pleasure at the sight of her in his bed. He looked over, realized Marc was behind her, his hands running over her fair skin. The sight of her in his bed, seeing his friend's pleasure as he touched their woman had some of the air backing up in his lungs. He knew now this was right, that everything he said had been correct. This was the right woman for them.

He cleared his throat, but his voice still came out harsh.

"Is it morning?" he asked.

"No," India said. She flicked her tongue over his nipple.

She moved over him then, wiggling between his legs, settling herself on her knees. Without preamble, she wrapped her small hand around his shaft. He felt the bed move as Marc got up, but Wade paid no attention to that. He couldn't. The woman stroking him had his entire attention. It was more than the pleasure she seemed intent on giving him or the way her hand slipped over him. The delight and power brightening her eyes held him captive.

Marc came beside the bed and pulled open his nightstand drawer. Wade glanced over and smiled when he saw the plug he retrieved. Wade bought it a week ago with India in mind. Her hand stilled, and he knew the toy had captured her attention. Marc grabbed a tube of lube and moved behind her on the bed. Neither of them would push her again tonight, but she did need to get more accustomed to anal play.

"India," he said.

She swung her gaze to his. He expected to see some fear. She was a novice, although he was sure both he and Marc would take care of that soon enough. Instead, he saw the flash of excitement flare in her gaze. His cock jumped in her hand, and she looked down it and then back up to his face. He smiled at her.

"Your enthusiasm is a turn on."

She shivered, her breasts swaying with the movement. Her nipples were already erect, begging to be touched. He reached forward and brushed the back of his fingers over one.

"Relax, honey," Marc said. Wade looked around her and saw Marc ease a lubricated finger into her anus. She shivered again and closed her eyes.

"Damn," Marc muttered. "She's so damn tight."

The need he heard in Marc's voice heightened his own. "Like a fist."

Marc continued to move his finger, and Wade turned his attention to India. "Hey, baby."

When she opened her eyes, stark hunger darkened her eyes. She lowered her head and took the tip of his cock into her mouth. She moaned against his cock as Marc eased the plug into her ass.

She raised her head, her eyes still closed and she moaned.

"You are such a delight," Marc said as he pulled himself up to his knees behind her. "It is hard not to pull that plug out of you and fuck your ass."

"India," Wade said as Marc slipped his fingers between her legs.

"Damn, she's dripping," Marc said.

"She gets hot faster than any woman we've ever had."

Marc looked over her head at him and smiled. Then he said, "Take his cock in your mouth."

India glanced behind her then back at Wade. She licked her lips before taking him into her lush mouth again. She tormented him, her tongue swiping out over the tip each time she retreated. Each time, she took him further into her mouth as she slipped her hand between his legs and dragged her nails lightly over his balls.

*Holy hell.*

She added her hand, pumping his cock each time she drew up on him.

She paused when Marc started to ease into her and moaned around his cock. Fuck, the vibrations moved over his flesh, shot through his blood, and caused his balls to draw up. He used all his control to keep from losing it right there and then. He wanted to come in her mouth, but not yet, not until both of them were with him.

Marc held on to her hips as he pumped into her. "Damn. I don't know how long…"

He didn't finish, probably couldn't and Wade understood. Being inside India was like heaven.

Wade slipped his hands through her hair, then pressed his palms against her head, easing her mouth back to his cock. She fell onto him hungrily, her enthusiasm almost overwhelming him. She took him so deep he could feel the back of her throat, but he controlled it, barely. Her moans increased, and her motions now became frantic as he felt her own arousal building. He watched Marc and India, watched the craving take over the two of them. Marc reached around and caressed her mound as she continued to assault Wade with her mouth. In seconds, she came, her body shivering with her orgasm. Marc came within moments, plunging into her as he shouted her name. Their pleasure undid Wade. India had recovered and worked his cock over, caressing his sac.

Marc pulled out of her at some point and lay down next to Wade.

"Come, Wade." Marc's harsh command pushed him over the edge. He thrust into her mouth, touching the back of her throat as he came, his orgasm pulling everything from him.

"That's it," Marc said. "Take it all."

She did as ordered, humming as she did. By the time she was finished, he felt drained as if he had been on a ten day hike in the desert. The woman would be the death of him.

"Come here, baby," Marc said.

She settled between them, and Marc leaned over to offer her a kiss. Something shifted between the three of them as he leaned in to do as his friend did. He looked up and saw Marc watching the two of them. He knew without asking, Marc felt the same about this as he did. Never before had it been about emotion…just satisfaction. But now, this woman, this night, would change their lives. They needed her…forever. Marc pulled her back against him, and Wade crowded in front of her. As he drifted to sleep, Wade promised that he would do everything to keep the three of them together.

* * * *

Marc came awake in degrees. He shifted his weight, trying to find a more comfortable position, and heard a mumble beside him. When he drew in a breath, he smelled cinnamon and magnolias.

*India.*

He opened his eyes and found her snuggled against him, her hand over his heart. Warmth filled his chest. He didn't expect this again, didn't want it. But the feelings he had for India were more than he'd had for Michelle. This went beyond attraction, beyond lust. This touched him down to his soul.

She mumbled something and moved closer. His cock jerked at the sensuous feel of her hardened nipple against his skin. Amazing that he had it in him, since they had taken her twice the night before, but Marc had a feeling that no matter how long they were together, she would have this effect on him.

Marc lifted his head and saw the bed empty beside India. Wade was always an early riser and apparently decided to leave them alone.

She huffed, her warm breath feathering over his skin. The hand that covered his heart now slipped down his chest, past his abdomen. A suspicious snort alerted him before her small hand wrapped around his shaft.

"India."

She rose, the sheets falling to her waist. The smile she offered him was filled with feminine satisfaction. A slant of morning light flashed over her golden skin and rosy nipples. The womanly confidence he recognized was both heartwarming and arousing. Every bit of moisture dried up in his mouth.

"I see that you're awake."

He chuckled, then moaned as she gave his cock a swift tug. She used her index finger to swirl around the tip, spreading the drop of pre-cum over the sensitive flesh. When she slipped her hand down to his balls, Marc jackknifed, then rolled over, trapping her beneath his body. His dick pulsed against her sex. Moist heat emanated from her core. She laughed. The sound of her joy lightened his heart, fed his libido.

She looked up at him with those Caribbean blue eyes shimmered with amusement.

I caused this, he thought with some wonder.

A sense of awe swept through him at the sight of her happiness. His hunger spiked. Her smile faded as she continued to look up at him.

"Marc?"

He shook his head, unable to explain what she did to him. How could he tell a woman that she turned him inside out? That until that very moment, he thought she was there for the both of them…together. Not separate. And just how did he tell her she made him believe again?

He bent his head and moved his mouth over hers. He didn't close his eyes, but continued to hold her gaze as he tasted and teased her. Soon, though, he could not hold back and slanted his mouth over hers, thrusting his tongue into her waiting mouth. Closing his eyes, he deepened the kiss, pouring every ounce of his need into it.

Moving from her mouth, he slipped down her body, pulling a nipple into his mouth, scraping his teeth over the tip. She moaned her pleasure as he pinched her other nipple. He slipped farther down, settling himself between her thighs. Her curls were dewy with her essence. The musky scent of her arousal filled his senses. He placed a hand over her mound and took pleasure in the moist heat that warmed his palm. He pressed hard, rubbing the heel of his hand against her clit. Her legs fell open wider.

"Marc." Excitement and need threaded her voice, spurring him on.

Knowing he couldn't wait any longer, he lowered his mouth to her pussy. The moment he slipped his tongue between her folds, the taste of her exploded in his mouth. Sweet, but tangy, an orgy for his senses. Marc drew her clit into his mouth and gently sucked as he slipped a finger between her folds. Her muscles surrounded him, pulling him into her warmth. Adding another finger, her moans increased. India slid her fingers through his hair, urging him on. Her muscles quivered then she exploded, convulsing as she screamed his name.

He kissed his way back up her body, ready to plunge into her.

"Dammit."

It aggravated him that he had to stop and grab a condom. In record time, he tore open the package and rolled it on. He turned to her and found her smiling at him, a look of lazy satisfaction in her gaze.

He slipped back between her thighs and entered her in one hard thrust. He had the pleasure of watching her eyes go blind with pleasure. Wanting to draw out their enjoyment, he moved slowly, building her back up again. Nothing ever felt as good as the way her inner muscles tightened on him, how her warmth surrounded him. Soon, she was frantic beneath him, her frenzied movements telling him that she was close again. He skimmed his hand down between their bodies until he found her hardened clit. One caress sent her up and over again. Ripples of delight pulled him deeper into her core.

She arched, screaming his name again. When she settled back against the pillows, Marc thrust into her, still trying to extend their lovemaking, wanting her to come again. But she looked up at him, her blue gaze filled with love. She brushed the back of her fingers over his cheek.

"Marc." He could barely hear her voice, but he saw her swollen lips move, heard the feeling behind it. It touched something deep inside of him, pulled at him, and he lost control. He drove into her once…twice…

He shattered, his orgasm washing through him, draining him, completing him. Everything he had, everything he wanted, poured into his release. He collapsed on top of her, his heart beating against her chest.

Long moments later, he was aware that her hands moved over his back, and he realized he was crushing her into the mattress. He rolled over onto his side, then pulled her against his chest.

Now that it was over, panic set in. He felt connected to her during sex, even before sex, but what now? Was she just in it for the fun, for the pleasure?

She pulled on some of his chest hair. "Stop worrying."

"What makes you think I am?"

She rose up to her elbow and smiled down at him. Her curls were a mess, and a light sheen of perspiration damped her forehead. Her smile was contagious.

"How can you worry about something as glorious as that was?"

The simple question, along with the joy behind it, made his chest ache. He brushed his fingers over her cheek in much the same way she did. She turned her head and kissed the palm of his hand.

"I need a shower." She slipped out of bed and smiled down at him, but now, there was a shyness to it. India was still not comfortable with her body. Her worries made her all that more human, and he felt his heart tumble down and slip right into love.

"I think we could both do with one."

Her eyes widened as he jumped out of bed and pulled her into his arms. She giggled as he walked her into the bathroom, the sound so wonderful, so perfect, he promised himself to try to get her to laugh every day for the rest of his life.

# Chapter Ten

India lounged on the massive sofa Marc and Wade had in their living room and sighed. Wade had her cradled against his chest as Marc rubbed her feet. There wasn't much a girl could complain about.

"If you keep cooking like that, I'll gain weight."

Wade chuckled. "I'm sure both Marc and I could figure out a way to work it off ya."

Heat filled her face as Marc smiled at her. "I think we're up to the task."

Something had shifted this morning. While Marc had been great the night before, she sensed that there was a bit of him he held back from her. This morning, though, she could see it in his eyes, see that he needed her as much as Wade. While he was the stoic one, the one who never seemed to need anyone, he might need her even more than Wade. Or maybe it was in a different way.

She settled against Wade and closed her eyes. Everything was so new, and she had no idea what either of them wanted out of this. If she thought too much about it, she might start wanting more. As in the whole nine yards.

Her eyes popped open. Jesus, she was thinking about permanent connections with two men when two days ago she thought to avoid a relationship with just one man.

"Something wrong?" Marc asked, his clear gaze roving over her face.

She knew she couldn't lie, knew he would sense her lies right off. So when the doorbell rang, she silently thanked God.

Marc frowned, but he rose from the couch and approached the door. It was a man, and India rose from the coach. When Marc returned, he didn't look any happier.

"Officer Daniels."

She smiled when she saw the young officer, hoping he had some kind of information for them.

His face flushed. "Ms. Singer."

"Why don't you have a seat? Marc, is there any coffee left?"

There was a look exchanged between Marc and Wade. Something was up, and she had a feeling they were hiding something from her. She didn't know what, but there was a good chance it had something to do with Johnny. Just the fact that they were trying to keep something from her pissed her off enough to put them in their place. Both Wade and Marc gave her identical grumpy looks. If she weren't so mad, she would laugh. But she would not act like the little woman who couldn't be exposed to the bad things.

"Ah...Ms. Singer, I don't have time for coffee."

"Okay. Was there anything you needed? Did you talk to Johnny?"

He looked behind her again, as if he was afraid Marc and Wade would jump him. She glanced back over her shoulder. They both had somehow made themselves look more intimidating. She narrowed her eyes.

"I think you can leave Officer Daniels and I alone for a moment. He isn't likely to abduct me while you're gone."

Both of them frowned harder, and while they weren't brothers, they definitely showed their unhappiness the same way. They wanted to argue, but apparently, they both knew better. They were already in trouble for trying to keep information from her and there was only so much she would allow.

Once she was left alone, she smiled at the officer again and motioned to the sofa.

He shook his head. "I don't really have time. We did pick up your husband. He had red paint in his car—"

"Red paint?"

He hesitated and swallowed. "I'm sorry, ma'am. I thought they..."

"Meaning Wade and Marc would tell me. Well, they didn't. Please tell me."

"There was some graffiti in your house."

Everything in her stilled, except her heart. That seemed to be beating so hard, she was amazed Officer Daniels didn't hear it.

"Explain."

"There was some paint on the walls."

She knew he was hedging, so she narrowed her eyes. His gaze slid away. "Would you like me to talk to your captain?"

He sighed. "The word 'Whore' was painted on the living room wall."

For a moment, she couldn't think. She had bad things happen to her and while she had not seen it, something about this made her feel dirty. As if the word Johnny had painted really applied. She brushed that away to deal with later.

"What else?"

"Your couch...it was ripped to shreds."

She nodded.

"Along with the brass bed."

She glanced up. "Tell me."

"He destroyed the mattress. Looked like he took a knife to it like he did your couch."

She shook her head as she tried to wrap her mind around it. This was just not like Johnny at all. He was passive aggressive, and while this wasn't actually confrontational, it was over the top. Like he had snapped.

Considering that Victor might be hunting him down, that was a very real possibility.

"Ms. Singer, should I call...ah..."

She realized then that the officer didn't know which man she was with.

She shook her head. "No. Is there anything else?"

"We picked up Mr. Anderson. He's been booked."

"Because of the paint."

"That and his prints matched ones found at the crime scene. I'm not sure how long they will hold him, but considering your situation, that he had a restraining order placed against him, that might keep him from making bail for at least a few days. They set it pretty high. He'll probably have problems getting someone to pay it."

She nodded. "Will you make sure to call me if he is released?"

"Yes. I made sure I would be kept up to date."

After thanking the officer and promising to come down and make an official statement on Monday, she let him out. For a few moments, she leaned her head against the door, closing her eyes. Jesus, her life was a mess. Her business was too new to call it successful, she was involved with two men who...well, she didn't know what to think of them.

As if conjured up out of thin air, they both appeared in the foyer. She could tell from the looks on their faces they both knew.

Without a word, she headed to the bedroom to grab her clothes. If her house was such a mess, she needed to get it put together.

"India?" Wade was the first one to break the silence. They followed her into the bedroom.

"You weren't going to tell me."

"We didn't think—" Wade tried to explain, but she was not in the mood to be lied to again.

"You're right about that one. Why did you think you had a right to keep that from me? And just how were you going to keep it a secret?"

"We thought that we could tell you when things had settled down," Marc said. "I guess we should have told you, but we had our reasons."

She placed a hand on each of her hips looking at them, waiting. "Well?"

"We wanted to protect you, and dammit, you didn't need to hear what that bastard did." Frustration dripped from every word. It was almost uncontrolled, so not like something Marc would do.

She looked at Wade, then back to Marc. "You didn't think I could handle it?"

Marc shook his head, but it was Wade who answered. "It's our right, and I would do it again. You looked so stunned by the break in that I just didn't want to expose you to it."

"You're right?" Her question came out in a lethal tone. Both men shared an uneasy look.

"What did you think this was all about?" Wade asked.

She frowned, confusion diluting some of her anger. "What was that all about?"

Wade sighed.

"What was going on between us...what did you think that was?" Marc asked.

Something tickled the back of her throat, and she cleared her throat trying to dislodge it. She tried her best to sound nonchalant. "I didn't think it was anything different than what you had done before."

Marc shook his head and walked toward her. She backed up a step. Something close to pain flashed in his gaze and he stopped, looking away. When he looked back, the unreadable mask she was used to seeing was back.

"I don't want you to be afraid of us."

Her heart softened. "I'm not afraid of you. Good Lord, do you think I would have slept with you if you frightened me?"

"Your ex—"

"Stop right there. Johnny was never abusive in the way you are implying, and I refuse for you to cop out to that. What I meant was that if you come near me, I can't think straight."

Wade snorted and she looked at him. "That's dangerous to tell us."

"So what? Your plan is to keep me tied to the bed and offer me constant sex so I won't argue with you?"

A silenced filled the room, the tension ratcheting up another level, this time definitely sexual.

She closed her eyes. "See what you two have done to me? I mean before this weekend, I never did or said things like that."

"I like the sound of that," Wade said.

She opened her eyes. "Give it a rest, Wade."

A muffled snort came from Marc's direction, and she gave him an evil look. His smile widened.

"Why don't you explain to me what you two mean by saying that you have a right?"

"We've been looking for a woman," Marc said, as if it explained everything.

She rolled her eyes. "Yes, I know, you share women—"

"No. I mean, yes, we do share women." Marc sighed, so obviously frustrated that she wanted to reach out to him. She wasn't used to seeing Marc so unsure of himself. "More Wade was looking for someone."

He glanced over at Wade, who said, "We want to keep you."

"What?"

"We want to have a permanent relationship, the three of us."

"Permanent?" Her voice turned strained.

"You shouldn't have blurted that out." Marc's voice gained some more of his authoritative edge again.

"Dancing around what you wanted to say wasn't working." Irritation dripped from Wade's voice.

"Stop it." She drew in a bracing breath. "You think we should date?"

Again, they shared a look.

"No. We said we wanted—"

"I know what you said, but I don't understand just what the hell you are talking about." Nerves that had been bubbling beneath the surface now rose to the top. "You don't know me. After one weekend with some sex—"

"Great sex."

She gave Wade a look that had him shutting his mouth.

"How can you know you want me? You barely know me. I thought you just wanted..."

How did she say she just wanted to play out a fantasy? She had known from the beginning that it was more than that, much more. But she didn't know if she was ready, if she could give herself over to one man, let alone two.

"A quick fun fuck weekend?"

Marc's brutal words made her wince.

"Not exactly, but I'm older, starting a business. And let's not forget having an ex who apparently slipped off the right side of reality. Why would you want me?"

Wade stepped forward and took her hand in his. "But I do know you, India. I know your dreams. I know what makes you laugh."

Marc stepped forward, effectively blocking her. "I know you are a damned smart business woman and you have a soft spot for the underdog."

"All we want is a chance," Wade said the words softly. She was shivering from the heat of having both of them so close to her, and fear.

"Just how would this work? I mean, I carry on with the both of you?"

"Why is that so hard to grasp?" Wade asked. "We want you, you can move in with us. There is a third bedroom, plenty of room."

Some of the shock must have shown on her face. Move in with them? She barely knew them, but that wasn't what she feared. It was the sharp tug of pleasure she felt when he proposed it.

"What about other people? You don't think people would talk?"

"If it gets to be a problem, you can marry Marc."

He said it as if it was no big deal. She looked at Marc, who nodded.

Oh, God, she wanted this. Wade touched her heart by constantly lightening her mood, and Marc, he made her feel so damned sexy. She looked at both of them, their sincere expressions, and said, "I have to think."

Wade opened his mouth, but she shook her head. "This is a serious choice. Would you expect me to make it quickly? You don't want me to have any regrets, do you?"

"You would never have any time for regrets."

She laughed. "Yes, I'm sure you would see to that in awhile. But I can't choose right now. My life is a mess, my house is a mess, and I am sure that isn't over. There will probably be at least an interview with the judge."

"I don't like waiting," Wade said it in the tone of a little boy being denied a gift.

"If you push me, my answer right now will be no."

A charged silence filled the room. She knew she was being weighed, that both men were trying to figure out which way to move next.

Wade looked at Marc, who nodded. Then Wade said, "Okay, we'll wait, but not for long."

# Chapter Eleven

"I told you not to rush her." Marc's quiet voice broke into Wade's thoughts.

"I know. I just thought—"

"You thought you would seduce her into bed and everything would be fine. That's exactly what I thought about Michelle, too."

Fear and irritation turned Wade's voice sharp. "Michelle doesn't come close to India."

Marc sighed. "No, not close. But you need to be ready for a rejection."

"What the fuck for? Why do I always have to plan for the worst fucking scenario? I'm sick of it. I want to look for something good in my life, something that I want to work out."

A beat of silence. "I know. I want—"

"What? You want what? You didn't think this would work. So if it fails, you can just walk away, again."

"Goddamn it. This isn't any easier for me. Do you think watching her walk out the door this afternoon was easy for me? I know there's always a chance she won't come back, that she'll just say we are too much, and every minute that she's gone, the fucking hole just keeps getting bigger."

Marc screamed the last of it. Wade was stunned. In all the years he had known Marc, he had never seen such a reaction. He closed his eyes, and Wade watched as his friend pulled himself back under control. When Marc opened his eyes, Wade saw nothing but pain.

"You don't think I know the consequences of her leaving today, but you're wrong," Marc said.

"I didn't say that. I said that I am sick of you looking at life as though you are waiting for everything to fall apart. Planning for the worst isn't a way to live."

"It is the only way—"

"No, dammit. It's not. I refuse to allow you to ruin this. India is ours. You know it has never been that good with anyone."

Marc shook his head.

Wade stood, his hands fisted by his sides. "You're afraid."

Marc's face went blank. "Are you calling me a coward?"

Some of the tension he felt drained, and Wade rolled his eyes. "Good Lord, no. What I'm saying is you're afraid of commitment."

"Commitment? Been watching Dr. Phil?" He sneered, but Wade could read between the lines. He hit a nerve.

"After Michelle, you became a fucking robot. No emotion, always cool."

"My cool head saved your ass in Afghanistan."

"Jesus, Marc, let it go. From the moment you dumped Michelle, you've been morose. You never look forward to anything. Sex was an outlet, not a joy."

Marc walked away from him, but Wade stopped him. "I don't want you to end up like your father."

He stopped. "I'm not."

Wade took a bracing breath. "What do you think all those antics in Afghanistan were, Marc? You risked your life, got a ton of medals, but did you think you'd survive?"

Silence.

"That's what I thought. You didn't care if you lived or died. Well, you son of a bitch, I do. You're my brother, and I'm damned sick of seeing you existing and not living."

Marc shook his head. "And you thought a weekend of good sex would fix it?"

"No, but I know a lifetime with India would."

Marc snorted. "That worked out well, didn't it?"

The starkness of Marc's voice told him everything he needed to know. Marc was in love with India the same as Wade was. If she didn't agree, he could save himself the pain. Otherwise, Wade was pretty sure Marc would be a broken man. Wade didn't know what would happen if his friend dug a deeper hole. He might just lose him.

"You wait. She'll call."

Without another word, Marc left him alone with his whiskey. He hoped that India didn't let him down.

\* \* \* \*

"You did what with whom?" Delilah asked India. Her eyes widened and her mouth hung open.

India chuckled, delighted that for once she stunned her friend. Delilah's tales were usually the stuff of fantasies, thanks to her stunning body and outrageous personality. Tall, athletic, Delilah gained attention by just walking in a room. The long, straight, black hair, mocha skin, and light green eyes made her unusual and stunning. She could have just about any man she wanted—and did on a regular basis. To have her so flabbergasted was quite delicious for India.

"Marc and Wade, you know the owners of T and J."

"I know what you said. I'm just trying to assimilate it in my mind." She closed her eyes. They popped open. "I think you have to start at the beginning."

So India did. She started with her first meeting with them, through the entire mess with Johnny, and then her weekend with them.

"Holy hell, woman. When you let loose, you really let loose!"

"Tell me about it."

"When you told me what happened, I thought this place would look much worse."

India looked around at the freshly painted walls and the fixed window.

"Wade and Marc did that. They even replaced my mattress. I told them I have renter's insurance, but they ignored me."

"Wait, they showed up here, fixed things themselves?"

"Yeah, well, the paint, and cleaning up. I thought to do it myself. They showed up bright and early Monday morning and worked on the paint."

"And you're here for what reason?"

India laughed, but then tears rushed to her eyes. "Oh, God. Sorry." She grabbed a tissue and dabbed her eyes. "I didn't mean to do that. I can't seem to stop."

Delilah reached over and slipped her hand over India's. When she looked up at her friend, she knew the unasked question. "I'm afraid. Two men...very virile, younger men—"

"Want you. Jesus, woman, don't let that asshole Johnny rule your life. Is there any reason, other than your worries about pleasing them, that you shouldn't be with them?"

"Other than the fact that there are two of them and most people would find that strange?"

Delilah rolled her eyes. "Fuck them."

India drew in a deep breath. "What happens if they dominate my life?"

"I don't think they'll do that." Delilah shrugged. "Besides, I don't think you would let them."

"Please, I let Johnny walk all over me. What's to say I won't let them do the same thing?"

"India, I've known you since high school. I saw what Johnny did to you, saw the way you ran around trying to please him."

"I'm afraid I'll do it again." She whispered it, fearing if she said it too loud it might come true.

Delilah shook her head. "From what you say about these guys, I take it they are big, very alpha." India snorted and Delilah smiled. "And you told them to wait. Have they asked again?"

"No. And they haven't tried anything for a week. I mean, at least not overtly. They did take their shirts off to work."

Delilah laughed. "Sounds to me like they demanded, and you said not until you make up your mind. The days of being walked all over are done for you, girlfriend."

She sat there, absorbed what Delilah said, her mind going back over their demeanor, the way they treated her. There had been kisses and comfort, all of which drove her crazy. She could tell both of them were holding back, and hurting, but they did it for her.

A lightness she hadn't felt in days filled her chest, warmed her heart. She couldn't stop the smile that curved her lips.

"Ahh, I see that you get it."

India looked at Delilah, her mind going back over her feelings for the men. Wade was wonderful, always making her laugh, making her heart light. Then he would look at her and she would lose all thought of anything rational. Marc, his serious looks and dammit…she was in love with both of them.

"I love them."

"Yeah, you do. I could tell the way you talked about them."

"No, you don't understand. The one thing I worried about was being able to love both of them."

Delilah took her face in her hands. "You have more love to offer than anyone I know."

"I'm going to call them."

Now that she made her decision, she couldn't wait. She was already hitting speed dial as Delilah grabbed her purse and headed to the door.

"I'll talk to you later. Call me, tell me how it goes."

She didn't even register the door shutting as their home phone rang. Marc answered on the third ring.

"India?"

"Marc? Is Wade there?"

"Yeah. Wade, get on the extension. Are you all right?"

"Yes."

"Hey, India, how you doing?" Wade's voice was soothing, but she heard the same thread of tension she heard in Marc's.

"I've come to my decision."

Neither of them said anything, and now she started to feel nervous. What if they had changed their minds?

"India?" Wade asked.

"Yes."

"What's your decision?"

"Oh, it's yes."

An audible sigh sounded from both men, as if they had been holding their breaths. Then Wade laughed.

"Hell, woman, you know how to make a man sweat."

She giggled and heard the door handle jiggle. Thinking that it was Delilah returning, she whirled around, a smile on her face. The moment she saw who it was, her blood turned to ice.

Johnny stepped into the room, shutting the door behind him. The smile he wore was pure evil. The gun he held in his hand was pointed at her chest. "Hello, India. I bet you didn't expect to see me."

He lunged at her, and she evaded, screaming into the phone, "Marc, Wade, call the police."

She wasn't so lucky the second time he attacked her. They went tumbling down on the floor, the phone falling out of her hand and skidding across the floor. The back of her head slammed against the wall. She lifted her head, trying to push him away, but bile rose in her throat, her vision blurred, and her world faded to black.

# Chapter Twelve

India came awake with a fresh slap to the face. She tried opening her eyes, but a bright light burned them and her stomach roiled. Her head felt as if it floated ten feet over her body.

"Wake up, India."

For a moment, she resisted. It fucking hurt when she opened her eyes.

"India, dammit."

In the next instant, she realized it was Johnny yelling at her. She couldn't remember much, but the attack rushed back to the forefront of her mind. She opened her eyes and swallowed as her stomach did another slow, uneasy roll.

"Ah, I see you finally thought to wake up. Get the fuck up. We need to get out of here."

She stared at this man she had loved, had built a life with...or thought she did. It had never been about them, but about him. And now, he seemed to have slipped over into some kind of madness. The cool, collected Johnny now wore the expression of a hunted man.

Without any help, she pulled herself up to her knees. Another wave of nausea hit her and she hesitated.

"Goddamn it, woman! What the fuck is wrong with you."

She shot the bastard a look, but his attention was glued out the window. It gave her time to study his appearance. He wore a suit that had seen better days. It was torn, dirty, and wrinkled. The neat freak had fallen to the wayside. Now his hair was greasy, his face smudged with dirt.

India pulled herself up completely and took stock of her injuries. Her head pounded where she hit it on the floor, and after a step, she realized she could function.

Now, he looked at her and sneered. "You never were that bright, were you? What the hell did you think would happen when I made bail?"

"I thought you would be smart enough to leave. Victor will get you, no matter where you go."

His face mottled with anger, his eyes bulging out of the sockets. He took two steps and then wrapped his fingers around her upper arm. The gun was now aimed at her belly.

"Stupid? No. I'll get out of here, but not before I take care of you and that pair of bastards you've been fucking."

"They'll hunt you down." She knew that without a fact. No matter what happened now, whether she lived or not, Marc and Wade would not rest until Johnny paid and probably with his life.

"Ha, you think they care about you? You're just another woman to them, one easily replaced." He sneered. "Whores are easy to find."

She opened her mouth, but she heard a car door slam shut, then another. Johnny dragged her to the window and smiled down. Marc and Wade were here, running up the walk to her front door. Johnny pulled the gun away from her body and took aim at Wade who was in front. Rage surged through her blood. She would not lose them, she would not allow this bastard to hurt them.

She grabbed his hand and pushed at it, using her body weight to send both of them falling to the floor. As they hit, the gun discharged. Her shoulder burned as she rolled away from Johnny.

The door burst open, and she thought she heard her name, and Johnny scream in agony. All of it blurred as the world slipped away.

\* \* \* \*

"Stop pacing," Marc said.

"I can't help it. If I don't pace, I'll go insane."

Marc sighed and said nothing else because he couldn't argue with Wade. Once they got to the hospital, the doctors hadn't been forthcoming with information. No arguing, threatening, begging got them any information. In the rational part of his mind, Marc knew that they had to wait. The wound wasn't bad, the bullet passing through, but he couldn't help it. From the moment he heard her on the phone screaming for help, his world had been shattered. Even in Afghanistan he hadn't felt such terror. The ride over had seemed like it had taken hours instead of fifteen minutes. His heart stopped the moment he heard the gunshot.

"That bastard got taken care of right away." He glanced at Wade who had stopped in front of him.

"Jesus, Wade, stop it. They had to treat him, and all he has is a concussion, which you gave him by pounding him into the floor."

"Gentlemen."

They looked at Officer Daniels, and he held up his hands. "He made bail. I told them to inform me if he did, but they didn't. I had no idea."

"Damn good that restraining order did her."

The younger man sighed. "Yeah, but this time, we have him for attempted murder, unlawful possession of a firearm...well, there is a long list."

"Mr. Jasper?"

Both Wade and Marc were up and moving toward the doctor. She was an older woman, gray sprinkled through her short dark hair. The dark brown eyes studying them looked weary.

"I'm Jasper."

She looked over at Wade. "And I take it you're Thompson."

Wade nodded.

"Hmm, lucky girl. She'll be fine. Bullet passed through. She lost some blood." Both of them opened their mouths, but she held up a hand. "No, she'll be fine with rest. I take it you both will make sure she does rest."

They nodded and she smiled at them. "Oh, to be twenty years younger. She'll be in her room in a minute or two. The nurse will come to get you as soon as she is settled."

When she left them alone, Officer Daniels cleared his throat. "We'll need to have official statements from both of you and Ms. Singer. I'm assuming she'll be staying at your apartment."

Wade said nothing, so Marc said, "Yes. She'll be with us."

When they were alone, he finally convinced Wade to sit down. After a few minutes, he asked, "Do you think she'll move in with us? Or that she even wants to be with us?"

The insecure tone was so out of character for Wade. Marc studied his friend. Apparently, today had really thrown him for a loop. Marc smiled. "She said yes earlier. And there is no damned way I am letting her go back to that house."

A grim frown was all that Wade offered him. His jovial manner was completely subdued. "But we didn't…"

Marc's own smile faded. "Yeah, we didn't get there in time." And that still burned a hole in his gut. They both knew they had done a piss poor job of protecting her. They hadn't been keeping tabs on Andersen.

"She has a right to tell us no."

Marc's smile returned. "Yeah, but that doesn't mean we have to listen to her."

\* \* \* \*

India came awake in a rush. The fresh antiseptic smell was the first thing she noticed. There was a beeping noise, the sound of some kind of monitor. Low murmurs surrounded her.

*Men…Wade and Marc.*

She knew without seeing them that they were there. It took monumental strengthen, but she lifted her lids and found two very worried men leaning down. Worry etched both their features and darkened their eyes. Her heart warmed the moment she saw them. They were safe and they were here.

"Hey, love," Wade said. "How you feel?"

His voice was barely above a whisper, but it sounded like he was yelling to her.

She swallowed. "Like I've been shot."

There was a beat of silence, then Wade's lips curved. "That sucks."

She tried to smile, but she wasn't sure she achieved it.

"It's nothing to laugh at," Marc said. When she looked at him, she noticed he wasn't touching her. He held himself back, and at one time, she might have thought it was because he thought less of her. She knew better.

She tried to lift her hand, but the energy just wasn't there. "Let me have your hand."

He hesitated for a second, then he slipped his palm beneath hers and brought it to his mouth. His lips glided over her fingers.

"Don't do that to us again." Marc's order came out in an anguished whisper that brought tears to her eyes.

"He was going to shoot one of you…both of you. I couldn't have dealt with that. I love you both too much."

His eyes brightened with surprise, and he glanced over at Wade. His expression held no surprise, only a self-satisfied smirk.

"India." Marc said her name as if it were a prayer. With care, he leaned down and brushed his lips over hers. It was sweet, almost platonic, but she felt the need behind it and the love.

"Get out of the way," Wade said.

Wade's gaze never left hers as he leaned in for a quick kiss. He rested his forehead on hers and his smile faded. "Don't ever do that again. Promise."

Now she didn't even try to hold back the tears as she nodded.

"Marc and I are going to be taking you home. You can't go home by yourself."

She sighed as he moved away from her. "That is really sweet, but I really don't think that's going to be possible. Besides, Delilah can help me."

Wade opened his mouth. Marc interrupted him. "I talked to her when she called your cell. This is not negotiable. You go home with us, final decision."

She was going to argue, but what was the use? And just how stupid of a woman was she that she would turn down two hunky guys who wanted to take care of her? Besides, Delilah was getting ready for her new job somewhere in the middle of West Texas.

"Okay."

Wade brushed a kiss over her forehead. "You won't regret it."

\* \* \* \*

Three weeks later, India was ready to scream. From the moment they brought her home, both Marc and Wade had hovered. At first, it had been reassuring. She felt so vulnerable and she needed that comfort. But as the days turned into weeks, she realized they were avoiding touching her.

"Are you trying to kill that tomato?" Delilah asked her.

India looked down at what she had done and grimaced. "Sorry. Just thinking."

"I hope not about me."

India chuckled and looked at her friend. She'd shown up every day and had been about the only thing keeping India sane.

"The guys."

"Yeah?"

"They won't let me do anything."

"What do you mean?" Delilah asked as she dumped her onions in the hot pan.

"This is the most activity I've had since I got out of the hospital."

"Really?"

Just then, Marc wandered into the kitchen and looked things over. "Everything going okay?"

Irritation marched down her spine. "Everything is fine."

Silence descended over the kitchen.

"We should have the pasta ready in about twenty minutes," Delilah said.

Marc offered Delilah a kind smile. "It smells delicious."

Delilah giggled—and that was the first time she ever heard her friend giggle like that.

India rolled her eyes. "Go away."

Marc looked at her with a knowing smile. Gently, he brushed his lips over hers, teasing her with just barely a taste of him. Before she was satisfied, he pulled away and walked out of the kitchen whistling a light tune.

"How can you complain about a man—correction, men—who treat you that well? I'm ready to conk you over the head and throw you into the river. What's wrong with you?"

"What's wrong?" She slammed down her knife. "Let me tell you what is wrong. Damn men. I cannot do a thing without them hovering, watching my every move."

"It's sweet."

"This from the woman who dumped a guy because he wanted to know where she lived."

"Hey, he could have been a serial killer."

"You slept with him and you thought he might be a serial killer?"

She shrugged. "He looked like George Clooney."

"Oh, good Lord." Giving up, India grabbed the bowl with the ravioli she made and headed over to the Viking gas stove. It was the first time they let her cook, and she was going to take advantage. The kitchen was a dream come true with a six burner stove, two ovens, and a subzero fridge. And they had refused to let her have anything to do with it.

"So, tell me, what's wrong?"

India slowly added the ravioli to the boiling water and sighed. "Nothing. You know I can't sit still for long, and they have been keeping me tied to the apartment since the shooting."

"When a woman complains about having two men dote on her, there is something wrong. Especially two who are so…hmm tasty."

"Like I would know." It was out of her mouth before she could stop it and she knew from the silence behind her that Delilah had heard it.

She stepped up beside India and looked over at her. "So, they won't…?"

"No! It is driving me insane." When she realized she had said it in a near shout, she lowered her voice. As if on cue, Wade appeared in the doorway, a concerned look on his face. Of the two, he had been the one who surprised her. He'd been an ogre, watching her every move, not allowing her to do anything.

"Is there anything wrong in here?" His tone told India that one word from her and he would throw Delilah out.

"No, everything is fine. Go away."

He tossed a look at Delilah then turned around and walked out.

"You have your hands full with those two."

"I wish. That kiss you saw was the most passionate thing they have done to me since I got here last week."

Delilah cleared her throat, twice. When India glanced at her, she saw that her best friend was trying to hold back the laughter.

"You wouldn't think it was funny if it were you." India pouted as she tossed the rest of the pasta into the hot water.

Delilah snorted. "Only you would get involved with two men and not be getting any."

"Bite me."

"Honey, you are going to have to take the first step with them."

India shook her head. "They won't let me do a damn thing."

"Then you are going to have to challenge those two. I have a feeling neither of them would back down from that."

"That's true, but I don't want to play games." It felt wrong, so wrong to even go down that path. "I want this up front. I mean, I already told them I wanted to spend my life with them."

Delilah grabbed her by the arms and turned her to face her. "Listen to the girl who grew up with three older brothers. They are scared."

"What do you mean?"

"They almost lost you. Men don't take kindly to that, and they really can't deal with the fear. They either yell at you, or they are overprotective. Just tell them what you want and don't back down."

\* \* \* \*

All through dinner, India thought about what Delilah said and what she needed to say to her men. Marc and Wade truly had not done anything wrong, but now with Delilah's comments, she knew they were afraid. Were they afraid to touch her sexually? They must be. She doubted either of them was happy with the situation.

After they said their goodbyes to Delilah, India wandered back in the kitchen but stopped short of the door.

"This is tougher than I thought," Wade said as he brought in a stack of dishes.

"Well, we have to wait. She was shot. You know how long it takes to recover from that."

"But how much longer?"

Figuring she heard enough, she stepped into the kitchen and said, "Yes, how long?"

Both of the heads whipped around at the sound of her voice. Silence stretched as both of them just kept staring at her.

"How much did you hear?" Wade asked.

"Enough to know you two are being stupid."

Marc almost growled as he walked toward her. The mean look in his eyes probably would have scared a lesser woman. The only thing it did was anger her more. Damn both of them for making a decision before discussing it with her. And that is exactly what they did.

"We talked it over and knew you weren't up to it. So we decided to wait."

She placed a hand on her hip and frowned at him. "And just when were you planning on doing anything about it?"

Neither of them said anything, but they continued to stare at her.

"So let me guess, you two had a long discussion and decided to ignore me when we got back home."

At the word "home" something flickered over Marc's face that she just could not decipher. "I've been wondering if you have lost all interest in me."

Wade snorted. "Not fucking likely."

"Then why..." She took a huge breath of air trying to get her courage up. "Why won't either of you touch me?"

Stunned silence filled the room after her outburst. The look of total shock made her feel better. Maybe Delilah had been right. They hadn't lost interest.

"You think we aren't interested?" Disbelief colored Wade's voice. "That is just asinine."

"What do you expect me to think?" She couldn't help asking the question and felt the flare of embarrassment and shame wash over her. She hated sounding needy, but she needed an answer, needed to know. "Did what happened disgust you?"

"Talk about asinine," Marc muttered.

Wade walked toward her, his expression gentle.

"Honey, why would you think we weren't interested? Because that ass hurt you. That has nothing to do with you."

"But he would have hurt you. I wouldn't blame you—"

"Just stop. That's stupid." Wade bit out the words, which told her a lot. The man was patient and easy going, but apparently he was irritated with her.

"We still want you." Marc's words were quiet but filled with conviction. "It's been killing us not to touch you."

"You want me?"

They both nodded.

"Prove it."

# Chapter Thirteen

The stunned look on both their faces told her she shocked them.

Wade looked over at Marc, who stared at her with such intensity she was amazed he didn't bore holes through her clothes. Heat shimmered on the air between the three of them. Even with them just looking at her, her nipples tightened against her bra.

A small quirk of Marc's lips told her that she had pleased him.

"Are you challenging us?" Wade asked, his voice colored with equal parts amusement and dark need.

"I guess I am." She offered him a mischievous smile and cocked her hip. "Of course, not sure the two of you are up to it."

Another growl emanated from Marc. When she glanced at him, she almost laughed. That is, if she hadn't been so turned on. Heat flared in his eyes as he studied her. Slowly, he approached her and started to walk in circles around her.

"Do you really think you should be challenging us?" The warning in his voice made her insides go all gooey. "I know we're up to it, but I just want to make sure you can take it."

The image his intense tone brought about slammed through her with so much force she was amazed she didn't come on the spot. She closed her eyes, remembered the feel of being between them. It was something she had lain awake dreaming of for days now. Alone, in a cold bed.

She opened her eyes and found Marc in front of her. He was so close she could feel heat pouring off his body.

"India?" His hard gaze spoke his need for her. She glanced at Wade who was studying them. His gaze moved down her body, and she could feel it as if he had touched her. Prickles of heat flashed over her flesh as he raised it once more to meet hers.

Her mouth was dry, her body combustible, her panties damp.

She returned her attention to Marc. "I can take anything you can dish out."

He crowded her against the doorframe and pressed his groin against hers. He flexed his hips, and she shuddered at the feel of his hard cock against her. She lifted her hands to his shoulders, but he moved away before she could touch him.

"No. You don't touch. You don't decide. You said you could take it, and we are about to find out."

He moved around her and said over his shoulder to Wade, "Bring her into your bedroom."

Wade gave her no chance to respond to the orders. Instead, he bent down and scooped her into his arms.

"Wade..."

He smiled at her. "Shh. Everything's fine."

He followed Marc into his room, then placed her on his bed.

"Take off your shirt." The command shot out from Marc like a whip. Instead of getting angry, the brutal tone had another gush of liquid lining her inner lips and dampening her panties. Heat wound through her blood. She hesitated, and he said, "Now, India."

She grabbed the bottom of her shirt and pulled it over her head. A rush of goose bumps rose over her skin the moment the cool air hit her heated flesh.

Marc came to her then. He brushed the backs of his fingers over first one nipple, then the other. They were already hard, aching, her breasts so tender she almost screamed when he touched them.

With ease, he hit the front clasp of her bra. The fabric slipped away, her breast pouring out into his hands. "Such beautiful flesh." He tweaked a nipple then stepped away. "Get rid of the rest of your clothes."

She stood and hurried to meet his demands, then sat back down, her legs together.

He shook his head and Wade chuckled.

"Don't be bad, India. Let us see that pretty little pussy."

Excitement skittered over her nerve endings at the tone Marc used. She knew he had it in him, had sensed it from the beginning. Marc liked to be in charge, and God help her, it turned her on to hear it in his voice. She did as ordered. Another rush of moisture coated her slit.

"Damn," Wade muttered. "She's dripping."

She quivered at the craving that filled his voice. To be so needed, so wanted, it overwhelmed her.

"You say you can take us both on. Are you sure?" Marc asked.

She nodded, unable to speak. The way both of them were looking at her robbed her of speech. It was if she were the only woman in the world for the two of them. It was then that it hit her. They did think she was the only woman for them. She had been ready to commit to them, but she had not thought that this was completely permanent for them.

"Why don't you take a taste of that pussy, Wade?" Desire darkened his voice.

Wade smiled. "Yeah, why don't I?"

Without another word, he slid to his knees in front of her and placed his mouth on her pussy. She was ready to come the moment she felt the heat of his breath, the swipe of his tongue. She closed her eyes wanting to revel in the feel of his mouth as he slipped his tongue between her folds. Heat gathered, tightened, the pressure in her pussy gaining with each thrust of his tongue. She could feel her orgasm there, just out of reach.

"Just one thing, India." She couldn't register that Marc was talking to her until he pinched one of her nipples. She opened her eyes to find him on the bed next to her, completely naked. His cock was hard, a drop of pre-cum wetting the tip of the angry head. She licked her lips wanting a taste, needing it. He pinched her nipple again. "You're aiming for a spanking."

Wade pulled away from her sex, and she almost groaned in pain. "I'd like to see that."

"Her ass gets so red. I plan on getting it nice and rosy while I fuck her ass tonight."

Wade laughed, then set his mouth on her again. His tongue slid up and over her clit. Her orgasm started to build, the tension becoming almost painful, but Marc stopped it.

"Wade, move away."

Wade did as Marc ordered, and she caught the smile the two men shared.

"Are you trying to torture me?" she asked.

Marc rubbed the backs of his fingers over her cheek. "There's no trying about it. You challenged us, and we *are* going to do it."

His warning sent another shaft of heat spiraling through her blood, warming her from the inside out. She opened her mouth, but he placed his fingers on her lips. "There is one hard and fast rule tonight. You can't come unless I tell you to."

She moaned and flopped back on the bed. "You're going to kill me."

Marc leaned over her, his smile seductive and loving at the same time. "Only with pleasure, love."

She laughed but ended up moaning when Wade slipped a finger between her pussy lips. She could feel her muscles clamp on to his digit as he moved it in and out of her. Again, her orgasm built, shimmered just out of reach before Wade pulled away.

This time, he was replaced by Marc, who moved her farther up the bed, then covered her with his body. He settled on his knees between her legs and lifted her hips. With one solid, hard, thrilling thrust, he was in her to the hilt.

"Oh, God." She could barely get the words out. Her pussy vibrated, pulling on his cock.

"Don't come."

His clear gaze captured hers, and he didn't let her break contact as he pulled out of her and shoved all the way back in. Slowly, he tortured her with easy strokes, rubbing his thumb over her clit every few thrusts.

Wade joined them on the bed, naked, his cock hard and wanting her. The thrill of having two men needing her and only her left her dizzy. Her heartbeat accelerated as he moved to her head.

"Suck him," Marc ordered.

She didn't wait. She opened her mouth and welcomed Wade's cock. Together, both men moved in rhythm. As Marc pulled out, Wade shoved his cock deep in her throat. The sweet-salty taste of him filled her mouth, and she could feel his head bump up against the back of her throat. Each time she neared her orgasm, Marc would change position. Frustration built with arousal.

Abruptly, both men pulled away. She moaned because this time, it did hurt. Every pleasure point on her body hummed, ached. She wanted to protest, but she didn't have time. Before she knew what was happening, Marc was pulling her up and Wade took her place. Marc turned her over and placed her on Wade.

"India." She lifted her eyelids and stared down at Wade, his eyes darkened with passion, his need for her easy to ready. She pulled herself up to her knees, and just as Marc had done before, Wade entered her, hard, swift, and to the hilt. She felt her muscles cling to his cock, pull him deeper.

"Jesus, Marc, she's wet."

Marc slid his hands up over her ass, squeezing her flesh. "I know. Damn near came the moment I got inside her pussy. Feels like heaven."

Wade groaned as he pulled out and thrust back in.

"Oh, God, Wade," she moaned.

"What is it, baby?" Wade asked, his voice breathless as he continued to move in and out of her. "What do you need?"

"I need to come."

"No." Marc said the word, short and to the point. But as he said it, his finger slipped into her anus, preparing her for his entry. The cool lube made her shiver, her anticipation growing. "I'm going to be deep inside this ass when you come. I want to feel those muscles tighten on my cock as I fill your tight little hole."

The hunger she heard in his voice almost sent her over the edge, but Wade stilled as she felt the bed dip behind her. Marc's cock poked at her entrance as Wade's hands pulled her cheeks apart.

"Shit," Marc muttered as he worked his shaft farther into her. Both he and Wade groaned as his slipped past the first ring of muscles.

"Good, huh?" Wade asked.

Now she felt full to bursting, both men into her to the hilt, their cocks pulsing against her inner muscles. Marc moved his mouth over her shoulder as Wade took her face in his hands and pulled her down for a hot, wet kiss. His tongue swept in as he began to move again. This time, they moved together, both thrust into her at once. The pleasure-pain they built had her shivering, begging for relief. Sweat poured off both men as they continued to work her, pushing her just up to the edge, but not allowing her to jump over. When she tried to change the direction, take over, Marc did as promised. He slapped his hand flat against the fullest part of her ass. The sharp sting shot through her right to her pussy and ass. It added another level of torture to the need pulsing through her.

He slapped her again. "You going to do as I say?"

She couldn't answer him right away. Too many emotions, the love she had for both men, the surrender she wanted to give to them and only to them, choked her. Tears streamed down her face as she opened her mouth. All the escaped was a moan.

He continued his slaps.

"India?"

She finally gathered up enough strength to nod and Marc relented.

Both men began to increase their thrusts, moving faster, harder. She thought she would die from the pleasure as she climbed to the pinnacle once more. Marc shifted behind her, then said, "Come for us, India. Do it."

She sobbed out their names as she came, her body convulsing, her pussy and ass pulling both of their cocks further into her body. Both men groaned, the sound so primal it touched something in her soul. First Wade stilled, his body bowing off the bed as he filled her pussy. A moment later, Marc followed, yelling her name as he came.

Long moments later, he collapsed on top of her, but she barely noticed. Her body felt used, spent, her mind pleasantly blank as she drifted into sleep.

* * * *

"India, baby?" Marc whispered. "Are you okay?"

She snuggled her backside against his growing erection and he groaned. It had been just over an hour since they all passed out. He knew that they needed to discuss things.

As he watched her lay between the two of them, Marc could not help but feel a wave of contentment and satisfaction wash over him. She was theirs, now more than she had been before.

"Wade, wake up."

Wade mumbled something and pulled India against him. "Don't wanna."

He nibbled on India's neck, and Marc knew just how she tasted. The sweet, sassy flavor of her flesh would always draw him. And he wanted nothing more than to take her again, watch her go over again, but they needed to make sure that the air was cleared.

"Wade."

His friend frowned then shot him a nasty look. "What?"

Marc lifted an eyebrow. "There are things we need to discuss."

Wade nodded. "India, we need to talk to you."

She rolled over onto her back and lifted her arms over her shoulder. Arching her back off the bed, she stretched. Marc's mouth watered at the sight of her pretty pink nipples on display. They were hard, begging for their hands, their mouths.

Wade cleared his throat, and Marc lifted his gaze to his friend's. The amusement he saw in his friend's gaze made him shrug.

"I didn't say I didn't want to have another go. I just said we needed to clear the air."

"About what?" India asked sleepily.

"Us."

She opened her eyes. Her soft, loving look made his heart turn over in his chest.

"Marc wants to be sure you understand what is going on here," Wade offered.

She smiled. "I think I have the hang of it. Although, I wouldn't mind another practice session."

Wade chuckled and Marc felt his dick twitch. She slipped her hand down his body and he had to grab it.

"No, you do that, then we won't get this settled."

"What is there to settle? We're together."

"We want this to be permanent," Wade said.

She glanced at Wade, then turned her attention back to Marc. "I know. We settled that before the shooting."

"No. You seemed unsure earlier."

She said nothing for a moment, then she looked again from Wade then back to him. "I am not good at relationships." Both of them opened their mouths, but she stopped them. "No. I had very few boyfriends, and my one long relationship was with Johnny. I thought maybe you were mad at me about what happened. I thought the reason you hadn't touched me was because you didn't want me."

Wade started laughing. "Honey, Marc and I have been barely keeping our hands off you. We just thought to give you time."

She smiled. "I figured that out." She placed a hand on each one of their cheeks. "I love you both. You make me feel so special, so loved, I just can't imagine life without you."

Wade turned his head and kissed the palm of her hand. "I love you, too."

She turned toward Marc, and he bent his head and rested it on her forehead. "I love you, India."

Then he kissed her, trying his best to pour everything into that kiss. She opened her mouth and he dove in. In just a few seconds, his heart was already beating out of control. When he pulled away, they were both breathing heavily.

"Hey, leave some of that for me." Wade pushed him aside and leaned in for a kiss himself. As he watched his best friend lose himself in kissing India, Marc's hunger grew.

By the time Wade drew away from her, he could tell that Wade and India were ready for another round as was he. But he knew they had one more thing to cover.

"India." Her blue gaze was clouded with passion and his own spiked. "You will live with us? Be ours?"

She nodded

"But," Wade said, "It might raise eyebrows."

She shrugged. "Not sure that matters. Besides, it's our own business. You're not trying to scare me off, are you?"

"No," Wade said, chuckling.

"You aren't getting rid of us that easily," Marc commented.

Her eyes sparkled. "Good, because you are both stuck with me."

Marc took her hand again. "We wouldn't have it any other way."

She glanced at Wade, who offered her a huge grin. "No way. You're ours."

"And we are about to prove that to you, in case our earlier lesson didn't," Marc said and was rewarded with a full, lusty laugh.

"I'm counting on it," she said as Marc covered her body.

Wade leaned over and brushed his lips over her. "We'll make sure to live up to your demands, every day for the rest of our lives."

India smiled at both of them as she slipped her hands up over Marc's shoulders. "I do like the sound of that."

Satisfaction filled Marc's heart as he bent his head to kiss India.

Now he knew she was theirs, for now and forever.

# THE END

**MelissaSchroeder.net**

# ABOUT THE AUTHOR

Born to an Air Force family at an Army hospital, Melissa has always been a little bit screwy. She was further warped by her years of watching Monty Python and her strange family. Her love of romance novels developed after accidentally picking up a Linda Howard book. From then on, she was hooked. She read close to 300 novels in one year and decided romance was her true calling instead of the literary short stories and suspense stories she had been writing. After many attempts, she realized that romantic comedy, or at least romance with a comedic edge, was where she was destined to be.

Influences in her writing come from Nora Roberts, Jenny Crusie, Susan Andersen, Amanda Quick, Jayne Anne Krentz, Julia Quinn, Christina Dodd, and Lori Foster. Since her first release in 2004, Melissa has written close to thirty short stories, novellas and novels released with seven different publishers in a variety of genres and time periods. Those releases included a 2005 Eppie Finalist, Three Capa finalists, and an International ebook best seller in June of 2005.

Since she was a military brat, she vowed never to marry military. Alas, fate always has her way with mortals. Her husband is an Air Force major, and together they have their own military brats, two girls, and an adopted dog-daughter. They live wherever the military sticks them, which, she is sure, will always involve heat and bugs only seen on the Animal Discovery Channel. In her spare time, she reads, complains about bugs, travels, cooks, reads some more, watches her DVD collections of Arrested Development and Seinfeld, and tries to convince her family that she truly is a delicate genius. She has yet to achieve her last goal.

She has always believed that romance and humor go hand in hand. Love can conquer all and as Mark Twain said, "Against the assault of laughter, nothing can stand." Combining the two, she hopes she gives her readers a thrilling love story, filled with chuckles along the way, and a happily ever after.

**Siren Publishing, Inc.**
www.SirenPublishing.com

CPSIA information can be obtained at www.ICGtesting.com
Printed in the USA
BVOW04s1201110215

387282BV00009B/243/P